Miracle on I-40

Miracle on I-40

Curtiss Ann Matlock

MIRA®

ISBN 0-7783-2223-8

MIRACLE ON I-40

www.MIRABooks.com

Printed in U.S.A.

First Printing: October 2005
10 9 8 7 6 5 4 3 2 1

For Mama, who taught me to read

A Crisp December Evening

It's the time of day when the coral sun gives way to a satin starry night. The huge letters of Gerald's Truck Stop have started to glow bright red in the darkening desert sky along Interstate 40, which cuts right through Albuquerque, New Mexico. The sign serves as a beacon for weary truckers trying to get in as many hauls as possible before Christmas Day, and for frazzled families making the long trek home to Grama's house, and for footsore mothers needing respite at the end of a long day of searching out the perfect gifts. Big eighteen-wheelers chug in and out of the wide fuel bays, while minivans and sedans stop at the gas station, and speakers up above each reverberate with Christmas carols.

The fluorescent lights of the restaurant shine out from the wide windows, promising warmth from the scene inside. Steam rises from the coffeemaker, and the bubbling punch machines give off a rather cheery yellow-and-red glow. Lights twinkle on the small plastic green tree at the end of the counter, and brightly colored piñatas hanging from the ceiling sway a bit whenever the front doors are opened.

A short, thick man in a white apron and with sleeves rolled up to reveal blue tattoos comes through the swinging kitchen doors, bearing a tray of pie slices. This is Gerald, the owner and somewhat compulsive pie maker. He goes to the lighted glass dessert case and puts the slices inside, saving one slice, which he plunks in front of a rather forlorn man sitting at the counter puffing on a cigarette. The man looks startled. His wide eyes follow Gerald, who sweeps on back through the kitchen door without an explanation. The man looks down at the pie, up at the swinging doors, and back at the pie again.

The hands of the Pepsi-Cola clock on the wall read

five-twenty, and there's a bit of a lull before the supper rush. In addition to the man at the counter, three elegant elderly ladies chat and laugh in the big corner booth, four truckers sit at a table talking low, and several other men eat alone, one a man in a suit who reads a paper, the other two robust truckers thoroughly enjoying their meals in the complete comfort of men used to eating alone.

There is only one waitress in evidence. She lifts the full pot of hot coffee from the Bunn machine and, swirling the contents, passes by her customers to refill cups. She casts repeated glances out the window, in the manner of watching for someone.

This waitress is a young woman, but not as young as she once was. Her hair is thick and wavy and the color of honey, and her eyes that particular green color of cactus in the spring. She is a pretty woman, like a thousand other pretty women, until she smiles. She has a smile so brilliant and so genuine that it actually, for brief seconds, arrests the recipients and causes them to stare. She smiles a lot, having learned that her ability to smile, even through her tears, is her greatest strength, the thing that has enabled her to not only survive but to enjoy life.

Lacey is the name printed on the small white tag above her left breast, and this is the story of a special Christmas in her life. It is a Christmas when she makes a choice to face wounds from the past and to hope in forgiveness. She doesn't know how much her choice, which seems comparatively small in the scheme of things, will affect those around her.

Right that minute, Lacey has paused at a table and is smiling at a big, rough-looking man wearing a Harley-Davidson ball cap and a bushy gray beard. In a voice that yet bears traces of down-home, she asks, "More coffee, Web?"

Web Connor, not a man given to much smiling, had to smile back at her, of course, although he shook his head. "No thanks. I gotta get goin' if I'm gonna make Okie City tonight," he drawled and began to slide his hefty frame from the red vinyl seat. "Gerald outdid himself on that dried peach pie today."

"I'll tell him you enjoyed it." Lacey picked up the bills he left atop his check. "You have a safe trip, and I'll see you again soon," she called after him as he wound his way among the Formica-topped tables to the door. Then she realized he'd left way too much money. "Web! Wait! You left this extra twenty." She waved the bill in the air.

At the door, the big man turned and called back gruffly, "You think I haven't noticed how you always get me the biggest slice of pie and make sure my steak's done just right?" He raised a hand. "Merry Christmas from me and Milly."

Lacey stood there and watched him push through the door and walk rapidly away toward his tractor-trailer rig he drove for Outtman Trucking. Turning slowly back to the table, she tucked the twenty-dollar bill into her apron pocket, where it seemed to burn a hole. She blinked back tears as she gathered the dirty dishes.

She paused and looked out the window, peering hard, but it was getting so dark now that she saw mostly her own reflection.

She breathed deeply and thought, Thank you, Lord, for people like Web. Thank you for Christmas. It's just a darn good idea.

Smiling to herself, she began to clear the dishes and to hum along with the jukebox. *I'll be home for Christmas...oh, yes, I will...if all goes well.*

As Lacey rounded the counter with her load of dishes,

the swinging doors burst open, and a middle-aged woman with a youthful air, curly blond hair, reindeer antlers on her head and the name *Jolene* embroidered in large letters above the chest pocket of her blouse, came through the door. "Doin' okay out here?" she asked, turning to adjust her antlers in the mirror that lined the wall back of the counter.

"Doin' fine. Not a creature stirring," Lacey said and glanced at the clock. Five thirty-three. She was to get off at six, having worked yet another ten-hour day, in order to get all the tips possible—although it was beginning to look like it might turn out to be a slow night. It was just as well. She was tired, and very thankful that this was her last day for two weeks. *If all went well.*

Every time thoughts rose up of what could happen with her plans, she imagined a radio dial in her mind and switched herself to a different channel, one where only happy and hopeful thoughts played.

She looked back at Jolene. "Someday you'll have to teach me your trick for keeping all the customers away from your tables and sittin' at mine."

"It's a secret I shall never reveal," Jolene quipped. "I employ it only when I'm tired and feeling generous—

you need the tips more than I do." Casting Lacey a saucy smile, she danced away to the jukebox.

Lacey idly watched the older woman and wondered what it might be like not to have to constantly worry about money. But Jolene had no children. Lacey wouldn't trade places with her, not for an instant. Well, maybe for an hour, in which time she would get a manicure and pedicure. Lacey had never in her life had either, and she thought about this as Glen Campbell's voice sang out from the jukebox about Santa coming to town, and Jolene wiggled her hands in the air, her Christmas-red fingernails catching the light.

Changing the channel on her thoughts, Lacey hummed along with the music and stacked dirty dishes in the pan to go back into the kitchen. She looked out the windows again and reached into her apron pocket to feel the folded wad of bills, letting anticipation steal over her.

"Does that guy always slide his cup back and forth like that?" Jolene asked when she had danced her way back behind the counter. She inclined her head toward where a lanky J. B. Hunt driver sat alone.

Lacey nodded and slipped the funnel from the coffee machine. "He has ever since he came in."

"Glad he's over there. If he was any closer, I think I'd scream at him." Jolene reached into the cabinet and plunked a box of coffee filters on the counter. "What is it? Your eyes are lit up like Christmas trees…like you have a secret."

Lacey couldn't help smiling broadly as she discarded the used filter. "I've made enough in tips to get Jon the remote-control car he wants for Christmas—the exact one. I've been putting off buyin' any other model, hopin' I could get the real thing."

"That's good, honey. And how are the kids? Are they getting excited about the trip?"

"Anna has a cold, and yes and no to excitement." Lacey rinsed the funnel. "I didn't bother with a tree this year, since we're not goin' to be home, and the kids were none too happy about that. Jon said he didn't want to go, if we couldn't have a tree at home. But on the whole, they both see the trip as an adventure. They've told everyone—and I mean everyone, including the UPS delivery man—that they'll be ridin' across country in a big eighteen-wheel truck. And they started askin' all kinds of questions about their grandparents and what things were like when I was a kid."

"Did you tell them about the problems between you and your parents?" Jolene asked.

"I tried," Lacey said, jamming the coffeemaker back together. "But every time I lost my nerve. I was afraid of prejudicing the kids against their grandparents or makin' them disappointed in me. They're both too young to understand it all, and I don't want Jon to think his grandparents didn't want him." She sighed.

"I ended up simply sayin' that Grandpa didn't know we were coming, and it was to be a surprise. If things don't go so well, then I can explain more. Maybe." She didn't really know how she would explain if her father rejected them.

"I guess it would be a pretty touchy subject," said Jolene, shaking her head. Then, "So, are you all set for the trip?"

At that moment the front double doors opened, and along with a whoosh of cold air came a family of four. With some disappointment, Lacey watched them head directly to the restrooms.

"I have a few last-minute things to get tonight," Lacey said, remembering to switch on the coffeemaker. "There's Jon's car, and nose drops for Anna, and new underwear for me. Why is it that women's panties don't seem to survive more than five launderings these days?"

"You could go without," Jolene suggested, studying a broken fingernail.

Lacey glanced at the clock and felt her stomach tighten. "I sure wish Pate would show up or call. He said he'd pick us up at the house at six in the morning, but I was expecting to hear from him today sometime, just to make sure."

"If Pate told you six tomorrow mornin', he'll be there at five to," Jolene assured her. "He's as punctual as the sunrise."

"I know."

Jolene regarded her thoughtfully. "Pate's a lot like my Frank. You could do worse."

"Oh, Jolene. It's not like that with us. Pate's more like a father to me."

"What do you think Frank is to me? Like a father and a lot more. Older men can give you what younger ones never can—in more ways than one, if you get my drift." Jolene gave her a knowing look. "It's a thought."

"No, it's not."

"Okay—don't get touchy. I'm just giving you the benefit of my own vast experience."

There could be no doubt in anyone's mind that Jolene had far vaster experience than Lacey, but Lacey refrained from speaking the comment. Jolene, and a few others, often said that Lacey didn't know the facts of life; Lacey thought that she knew them only too well, and managed to rise above them.

The man at the counter waved his check at them, and Lacey moved to the cash register.

"Uh…that cook gave me a piece of pie."

"No charge, then." She thought he was a very sad-faced man, and made the effort to give him a particularly warm smile.

The man gazed at her, as if he didn't comprehend.

"He does that—gives out free pie when he feels like it. You liked it, didn't you?"

"Uh…yes. It was very good." He came close to a full smile, unable to help himself.

"Now maybe you'll order one again."

"I don't think so. I'm on my way to Louisiana. I don't have plans to come back this way."

"That's okay. If you ever do, you'll order the pie, and you can tell your friends about it, too."

"Yes…thanks."

"God bless you for your trip home," Lacey said, impulsively. He seemed to need it.

He looked a little startled, and then he smiled a small but true smile and turned toward the door, drawing his coat up around him. Lacey watched him for a long minute, then swept a gaze around the parking lot, bending to peer as far as she could in each direction.

People all coming and going, all with their own pocket full of hopes and dreams and needs, she thought.

The family of four had emerged from the restrooms and chose a booth in Jolene's station. Their expressions had lightened, no doubt reflecting anticipation of delicious food. Jolene looked from them to Lacey, sighed deeply, and got a tray to carry water glasses. Then she pointed discreetly at the door. "Mmm, he's a sight to warm a woman's heart…and he's comin' right to your counter, you lucky gal," she whispered as she took up the tray and started away.

Lacey saw the sight to warm a woman's heart was a customer they all knew as Cooper, pushing through one side of the glass doors. A tall, lean man, he came through the door without opening it all the way, his head tilted downward just enough to conceal his eyes with his cowboy hat.

Lacey reached for a menu, even though it was probably a waste of time. She had been serving the man for some years now, and he either ordered the Texas T-bone or the Piping Hot Chili, always topping off with a piece of pie and ice cream.

And thinking of this, she remembered that he always sat in a booth, usually a front corner one all by himself, with a good view of the truck parking lot. His coming to the counter was unusual.

"Good evening," she said in her friendly customer voice. She set the menu in front of him, then glanced up and found herself looking into his dark eyes. He had an odd expression. A hesitancy? A nervousness?

Cooper, who did actually feel nervous and was blaming his discomfort squarely on Lacey Bryant, extended the folded piece of paper and said, "From Pate." He figured the note would explain, so he didn't think he needed to say more at this point.

The gal's pale, slim, feminine fingers seemed a stark contrast to his large, rough, dark ones as she slowly took the note. Confusion and apprehension clouded her eyes. Cooper noticed they were the color of spring grass just before she lowered them to the paper.

He ran his gaze over her glossy hair and ivory cheeks, and for the hundredth time, he asked himself how he'd gotten hooked into doing this.

Maybe he would escape his own foolishness. Maybe she would simply refuse to go.

Either she was a slow reader, or she couldn't comprehend the note the first time, because it seemed to take her an inordinately long time to read the few words. Cooper knew what was in the note; he'd read it, unashamedly curious about the exact nature of his friend's relationship with this young woman.

Dear Lacey,

Cooper will explain about me. He will also take you to North Carolina right along with hauling my payload on up to D.C. Cooper is a good man. I trust him with my life. So I can trust him with yours, too. Have a good Christmas. Hope everything turns out the way you want.

Love,
Pate

Cooper felt a bit of embarrassment over the high praise. And he wondered about it. He didn't think anyone, even a friend like Pate, knew him well enough to form such an opinion.

After what seemed like a very long time, the gal raised her eyes to him. Her face was white, her green eyes filled with confusion. "What…" She stopped and waited.

Just as Cooper opened his mouth to explain about Pate, a tall, good-looking sort of guy in a nice suit appeared at the counter near the cash register.

"Excuse me," she said, and stepped over to take the man's payment.

Cooper, annoyed at the interruption, observed the two. The guy called her "honey" and attempted to chat in an overly familiar way. She smiled at him with the same friendliness she gave everyone.

She wasn't what could be called a flirting type. Cooper, running his eyes over her, tried to come up with what type she was, and couldn't.

He had been coming into Gerald's and sitting at her table for over two years, maybe even three, because she was a darned good waitress. And also because she was easy to look at, but kept things cool. He had a couple of times even considered asking her out, before coming to his senses. She was one of those women a man didn't want to fool with. He wondered again about the seriousness of her relationship with Pate. Maybe Pate was the reason she didn't flirt. He and Pate never had talked women; they each liked a lot of privacy. And he had always sort of figured neither of them had a lot to talk about where women were concerned.

Finished with the customer, she returned and gazed expectantly at Cooper. "What's this all about?"

"It iced up on us in Santa Fe yesterday evening. Pate slipped and fell down the front stair at his apartment." He watched distress replace the confusion in her eyes. "Broke his leg bad enough to require a hospital stay. I told him I'd haul his payload and take you on to this place in North Carolina."

"Pine Grove."

"Yeah. He said west side of Raleigh."

She nodded, frowning and searching his face. Maybe now she would say she wouldn't go. Cooper waited.

The next instant, she turned right around from him and went to the back counter. He had a moment of confusion, wondering if he should call out to her to come settle the matter. He watched her get a mug and the coffeepot, and then she returned to thunk the mug on the counter in front of him, filling it with coffee, as she said, "Pate's in the hospital then?"

Cooper nodded. "Yep." He automatically reached for the sugar. "But he should be released day after tomorrow. His son and his son's family are flyin' out from Richmond to spend Christmas with him and take care of him." The sugar came out faster than he had anticipated. He spilled some on the counter.

"Oh." She was staring at him, but she didn't offer to wipe up the sugar, just stood there holding the coffeepot and looking at him.

He stirred his coffee, then said, "I'll have the chili dinner…and I'll sit over there." Slipping off the stool, he inclined his head toward the corner booth, then headed for it, wishing the gal would simply get to saying that she had changed her mind about the trip.

As he slid into the booth, he looked into the night-dark window glass and saw her reflection back at the counter, standing there gazing over at him.

"I don't know what to do now," she said to Jolene in a low voice, not wishing to have her business spread out to Gerald and the cook, both busy near the stoves.

She looked down to see that she was so flustered she had put tomatoes and cucumbers in the salad bowl, without the lettuce.

"So what's the big deal?" Jolene asked.

"The children are countin' on going." She got another salad bowl and filled it with lettuce. "They need to meet their grandparents and aunt and uncle and cousins. Their family. My sister and mother are plannin' on us being there Christmas Eve.

"I got myself all set to go home and face Daddy," she added, feeling near tears.

"So...go, honey," Jolene said. "Cooper said he'd take you."

"Cooper isn't Pate. Pate...well, we're good friends. I wasn't imposing on him—it's not imposing on a good friend. You didn't see Cooper's face. He doesn't want to do this. He's only doing it for Pate." She dumped dressing over the salad.

"So what? Doing it for Pate's a good reason. And don't pay any attention to Cooper's attitude. He always looks grumpy. The man's afraid to be friendly, afraid people will find out he's got as big a soft spot as everyone else." Jolene, who was mixing the house dressing, licked her finger.

"Where did you get that idea?" Lacey asked and handed Jolene a soapy dishcloth to wipe her hands.

"I've been serving him for four years. I've even been out with him."

Lacey stared. "When?"

"Oh, long time back. Maybe right before you came to work here. Before I met Frank, obviously." Jolene passed Lacey a small bowl of the dressing. "We went out twice, as a matter of fact. Once to a show, then to a show and dinner. He's a real gentleman—good manners and all, so you don't have to be worried. And he's a loner. He's not the marrying kind—he doesn't want any entanglements. He'll keep his distance. You will be perfectly safe."

Lacey gazed at Jolene. "Is Cooper his first or last name?"

"Well, I don't know." Jolene shrugged.

"You went out with him twice and never learned his first and last names? Didn't you ask?"

Jolene said, "He's just Cooper. Everyone calls him Cooper. Maybe that *is* his first and last names. And why would I need to know? Two shows and dinner doesn't mean marriage."

"I know Pate respects him," Lacey said, more to herself than to Jolene. "But I don't really know anything about him." She'd felt his low-key interest on a couple of occasions, but she didn't think she wanted to speak about this to Jolene.

"I think Pate's recommendation should be enough." Jolene pointed a finger at Lacey. "Cooper says he'll take you. You want to go home—you need to go home. Now's your chance, and my advice is to take it, because you're not gonna get another like it. Besides, what will you tell the kids? Sorry, it's all off? Then they'd have to tell their friends, and the UPS man, that their braggin' was all lies."

"Thanks, Jolene," Lacey said dryly and thrust the bowl of salad toward her. "You take this to him. I need a few minutes to think this thing through."

Jolene looked at the salad. "I hope he likes ranch dressing," she said as she walked away.

Lacey went to the cooler and brought back one head of lettuce and one of purple cabbage, and began chopping them with a cleaver, hard, swift chops. She thought of Pate. Pate Andrews was around fifty, widowed and lived alone, and seemed to love his truck as one would a wife. He had alluded to regret at paying more attention to his truck and trucking than he had to his marriage and family. He had one son, who lived in

Richmond with his wife and children, and the two were somewhat estranged. Pate had mentioned that he felt he was too rough for his son, who had been his mother's child. Sometimes Lacey had the idea that he sought to make up for the loss of his wife and family with his relationship with her.

Pate came into Gerald's on a regular basis, and over the years he and Lacey had formed a special kind of friendship. Pate had taken the place of the father she didn't have, the grandfather the children had never met. Her traveling with him out to North Carolina had been Pate's suggestion in the first place. He'd first mentioned it back in the fall, and the idea had lodged in her mind, popping up again and again, so that she had begun to imagine going home and making peace with her father.

When Pate had told her that he planned to get a payload to take him east to spend the holidays with his son, it had been easy to ask if the invitation to go with him still held.

"You bet it does, gal," Pate said immediately. "We'll make this a holiday to remember, both of us makin' a long overdue trip to family."

Everything had fallen into place. She had sort of

thought the opportunity had been a gift from God, a sign that she was meant to go home at last.

And hitching a ride was the only way that she and the children could make the trip. She could not afford a round trip, even by bus. A single mother with two children and a patched-up '77 Delta 88 that she couldn't possibly trust to carry them ten miles down the interstate, much less some eighteen-hundred-plus miles. What emergency money she had managed to put aside had been used up by the dentist for Jon and a new starter for the car. Her sister, Beth, had sent some money and wanted to have their mother send more, but Lacey refused. She couldn't come home to her father like that.

Besides, Pate welcomed their company, and she felt they were contributing to his holiday, too.

She was fairly certain Cooper wouldn't welcome their company, she thought, stepping to the double doors and peering through the small window, seeing him at his table eating his salad.

"Ridin' in a big rig? Man alive!" Jon had said. And, curiously, *"Does my grandfather know what I look like?"*

Anna had said, *"I'm makin' a pot holder for our grandmother."*

"Chili's up!" the cook called.

Lacey turned and walked over to get the steaming bowl, assemble it, the fresh bread Gerald had made, and butter on a tray.

"Mama's aging, and Daddy's heart could go anytime," Beth had said.

Jolene burst through the door, bearing the big plastic dishpan. She set it on a counter and whirled to hold out several bills toward Lacey.

"Here's your tip from that man who favored sliding his cup around. He was right nice, too. Now, you'd better get that chili out there to Cooper. It doesn't take long to eat that small salad…and no, I'm not takin' it. I've got to go do something with these antlers. They're givin' me a headache." And she went off toward the ladies' room.

Lacey lifted the tray of food, took a deep breath and pushed through the swinging doors.

As she walked toward Cooper in the booth, her heart thudded. He had to have heard her footsteps, but he didn't look up from the newspaper he was reading. Maybe he didn't hear her. She stood at his table a moment, looked at his thick hair. Goodness, it was glossy brown. His mustache was, too, and tinged with red, just like the hair on his head. And his eyes were brown as buckeye seeds.

She realized suddenly that he was looking up at her.

He folded the paper, wrinkling it in his haste, and she sat the plates in front of him, saying the chili was a little on the spicy side today, chatting in her nervousness.

She stood there, uncertain, rubbing her hands together. Then she slipped into the seat opposite him. His eyebrow came up. He gazed at her a moment, then looked at his bowl and sprinkled cheese over his chili.

"How did Pate seem when you left him?" she asked.

"He was wide awake and flirtin' with the nurse." He glanced at her, then stirred the chili, jabbing in the melting cheese.

"How long will he have a cast on?"

"Eight weeks, at least, the doctor said." He took up the bottle of dried pepper and shook it liberally over the chili. Without first tasting it, Lacey noted with a small bit of alarm.

"I'll get you a glass of water," she said, when she realized he didn't have one. She'd been negligent—they always brought the customer ice water first thing.

She hurried around the counter and got the water, and as she brought it back, the father of the family of four held up a finger and called, "Oh, Miss…Miss, we'd like to order pie to go, please."

She set the glass of water in front of Cooper, stepped away, only to stop and abruptly return to put a napkin under the glass to get the drips, then rushed to get pie for the family who were in a hurry to get on the road. After that she had to attend the register for a trucker and the elderly ladies, who wished her and everyone in the room a very merry Christmas, and get menus for two truckers who came in.

Jolene had apparently gotten very involved with her antlers. Surely Paloma, who was supposed to work the supper shift, would come in any minute, she thought, heading back to Cooper's table with the coffeepot.

"You goin' or not?"

Cooper's voice startled her, and she splashed the coffee out of his cup. "Oh…I'm sorry." She dabbed up the spill.

They gazed at each other.

Again she slipped down into the seat opposite him.

"I know it's an imposition, and I really hate to bother you, only…"

"Look," he said, holding his knife like a pointer, "I told Pate I'd take you. The deal is still on, just like before, and I'll probably get you there a bit faster than Pate would have. I don't make a lot of stops. It's not like it was with Pate—I ain't Pate—but it *is* a ride. Now, do you want to go?"

Lacey stared at those buckeye brown eyes.

"I'd be very grateful for the ride," she said.

He nodded. "Okay." And he looked down at his chili and scooped a spoonful into his mouth, hot chili and hot pepper.

Lacey sat there, gazing at him.

After several long seconds, he looked up at her with a raised eyebrow.

"Pate was going to pick me up at home at six o'clock tomorrow morning." *Why did this man have to be so purposely disagreeable?*

"You be here at the restaurant at five, and we'll head out." He returned his attention to his chili.

Lacey opened her mouth, then closed it. "Fine," she said at last.

Rising, she walked straight-backed across the room and through the swinging doors. *Oh, Lord, why did you let Pate break his leg?*

The Heart's Desire

At the exact moment that Lacey prayed for Paloma to arrive, the young woman came bouncing through the door, her arms laden with shopping bags, and singing "Feliz Navidad."

Lacey said, "Merry Christmas to you, too, my tables are all yours," and whipped off her apron and unpinned her name tag.

Growing a little frantic, with all she had to do racing through her mind like a pack of dogs chased by the dog-catcher, she got her coat and purse, even before asking Gerald if she could go.

"Feliz Navidad!" Paloma called to her.

"Honey, make it a good one," said Jolene. "I love your face…here." Jolene passed her a small black satin cosmetic bag. The name Estée Lauder was printed on the side.

"We agreed—no buyin' gifts." Lacey pushed the bag back at the woman.

"I did not buy it. It came as my free gift for buyin' the miracle wrinkle cream. Honest. Take it and enjoy."

Jolene gave a her a hug and a kiss. Gerald appeared with a pecan pie covered in plastic. The two of them waved her away at the back door, their wishes for a good trip and Merry Christmas echoing into the crisp dark night. Lacey hurried out past the Dumpster and a beat-up Rambler with someone sleeping in it, and over to her old white sedan, which looked even more run-down in the silvery glow of the parking lot lights.

She got in, set the pecan pie carefully on the passenger seat and pulled her coat collar up around her neck, because the driver's window was stuck down, which was why Anna had caught cold in the first place.

At the turning of the key, the engine protested with a lot of whines and grinds, snorts and pops, while Lacey whispered, "It will start…it will start…it *will* start." It did, and Lacey revved it several times, then backed out of her space and headed in a chugging fashion past the restaurant.

In the way of Universe arrangements, at the particular moment of Lacey's passing, Cooper was coming out from the restaurant and heading for his rig, where he intended to spend the night. He saw the car jerking along with clouds of smoke puffing out the back of it. Next, with some surprise, he saw the gal—Lacey Bryant—at the wheel.

He watched the pitiful car continue on to the entrance, where it paused before pulling out onto the narrow blacktop highway headed for town. It let out a loud backfire, then picked up speed and roared away.

Cooper, hands stuffed into his coat pockets, strode slowly on to his truck, wondering about her, and wondering about himself, and maybe, reluctantly, a little pleased he would have the gal's company for the drive east.

As soon as he realized the sense of pleasure, though, he stopped it.

The shopping mall was packed, people scrambling for bargains in the last days. There was only one Tough-

Stuff radio-controlled car left at the hobby shop. Lacey spotted it, and at the same instant saw another woman heading directly toward it.

With a burst of speed, Lacey sprinted and reached the car first, snatched up the box from the shelf and held it close. The woman glared at her, and Lacey's cheeks burned from shame.

"My son...he really wants this one, you see. He hasn't asked for another thing...and...I just have to have this one."

The woman's expression turned wary. She stepped back, clutched her purse to her bosom and edged away.

Lacey looked down at the box she held and then at the woman. *Oh, Father, find that woman another car.*

Then she turned resolutely to the checkout counter, and her embarrassment eased into joy as she handed her hard-earned money to the cashier. "My son's goin' to be so excited about this," she told the girl, who smiled brightly but, being only a young teen, could not possibly understand what it meant to a mother to want to please her firstborn son.

Walking out of the mall, Lacey looked into the shopping bag several times, reassuring herself that she did indeed have the car. She held the pleasure to her, which in part made up for the fact that she could not give Anna her longed-for Christmas puppy. But when they got back home after the trip, she promised herself, she would see about a puppy, even though it made not one bit of sense to take on another mouth to feed and one more to clean up afterward at the end of a long day.

From the shopping mall she drove to Wal-Mart, where she locked Jon's car in the trunk and raced into the store, tossing a couple of bills into the Salvation Army kettle without pausing and pushing a buggy down the aisles and around other shoppers like a marathon runner.

When she got back to her car, she threw her packages in the back seat with an audible "Whew!" Her feet and back ached, her hands were stiff and dry, and at home were two children to wash and stuff with a snack, before finishing up the packing. She never had been able to pack until the last minute.

It began to rain, and the Delta's windshield wipers squeaked back and forth.

"The traffic lights blinked a bright red and green…" came the holiday song over the radio.

She reached over and touched the bags in the seat beside her, beginning to worry about having overspent. But Anna had really needed socks, and that fancy hair clip hadn't cost *that* much. And Jon's present shoes were disreputable.

But she really hadn't needed to buy that belt buckle for Cooper. It had been a silly, extravagant thing to do. Fifteen dollars, on sale. It was the sale tag that had gotten her. For fifteen dollars, she could buy supper on the trip for her and the kids.

It's Christmas, came the whisper. *I will have enough money…I will have enough money…I will have enough….*

As she pulled into the driveway of her duplex apartment, the door opened from the adjoining apartment where the children stayed during the school break with their neighbor, Susan Price, who had her own baby on her hip and a toddler clinging to her leg. Ten-year-old Jon and five-year-old Anna came running to meet her, Anna throwing herself on Lacey, and Jon slipping his arm around her.

"They had hamburgers for supper," Susan told her.

"This one had two," she said, her hand affectionately placed atop Jon's head.

"Growin' boys have to eat," said Jon righteously.

"I'll be needin' to pay you for three mouths, instead of two," Lacey said, passing Susan the envelope she had prepared. "Thanks for takin' care of them for me."

"Jon's really a help to me, you know. And I had plenty extra. Marty's workin' late, again…you want to come have a hamburger?"

Her friend looked tired and lonely, but Lacey declined. "I've still got packin' to do."

Everyone called, "Merry Christmas," back and forth, and at last Lacey got herself and her brood into their apartment and closed the door. She felt an immediate relief, as if shutting out the world.

Then Jon and Anna were tugging on her, pretending to try to peek into the bags.

"You'll spoil your Christmas," Lacey cautioned.

"Not me. I won't see my puppy until Christmas mornin' after Santa brings it," Anna said flatly.

Jon switched on a lamp and threw himself on the couch, saying, "I've told her and told her that Santa won't bring her a puppy this year because of the trip."

"He might." Anna jutted her little chin.

"Pate won't want a noisy, messy puppy ridin' all the way back here in his truck from North Carolina." Jon sent Lacey a look; he was doing his best to help.

"He won't care," Anna said, her voice cracking.

"Let's just let the speculation drop and deal with what happens when," Lacey said, as she sat to remove her shoes and massage her feet. "You two need to get your baths and get to bed. Come on…"

She set Jon to packing his things, while she got Anna bathed. After Jon had gotten his bath, too, she had hot chocolate and decorated sugar cookies waiting for them. As they all sat around the faded green Formica table, she explained about the change in transportation plans.

Anna played her cookie around in her cup of chocolate, but Lacey felt Jon's careful attention.

"So…is Cooper his first or last name?" Jon asked. "Do we call him Cooper like we call Pate, Pate, or are we supposed to say Mr.?"

"Just say Mr. Cooper," Lacey told him.

"Jon…music off." She switched off his boom box, kissed his head and turned out the lamp beside his bed.

"Mama, what will we do with the puppy Santa brings?" Anna asked as she crawled into bed in the next bedroom. "Will Mis-ter Cooper let us bring him home in his truck?"

"Blow," Lacey instructed, holding a tissue to Anna's tiny nose. Anna puffed up and blew hard, took the tissue in her own tiny fingers and wiped her nose, then handed the tissue to Lacey and looked expectant, waiting for an answer.

Lacey stroked the fine brown hair from her daughter's forehead. "Anna, I told you that your puppy will have to come later, even if we were ridin' with Pate. A puppy is a delicate thing for Santa Claus to haul around, especially from the cold North Pole. Why, I can't think of anyone who ever got a puppy for Christmas."

"Tammy Henderson did. She said so today." Anna's big brown eyes dominated her face.

"Well, we see," Lacey said, regretting the words as soon as she said them, because she'd always hated to hear that as a child. "Now, you have to get to sleep, sugar. I'm goin' to have to get you up very early."

She tucked her daughter down in the bed and whispered, "I love you" in her ear just as she had every day since Anna had been born. She pulled the bedroom door to, leaving a crack for comfort, probably more for herself than for Anna. She stood there a moment, squeezing her eyes closed against tears. So often she felt inadequate in her role of mother.

Blinking hard, she pushed herself down the short hall and into the kitchen, where she poured a cup of coffee, carried the phone to the table and called Information for the number of the Santa Fe hospital. Her heart jumped when she heard Pate's voice, sounding perfectly normal, boom across the line. He had such a big voice.

"Well, hiya, Suzie-Q." He often called her or any other female Suzie-Q. He was obviously surprised and touched to hear from her, and kept repeating that he was fine. His son, Bob, was coming with his entire family, and they were due in the following morning. His voice echoed with the excitement of it.

"I never imagined that he'd come all the way out here," he said. "He's pretty busy with his law practice…and you know how things have been between us since his mama passed on. But soon as he heard the situation, he said he was comin', no two ways about it. We're gonna have us a grand old time after all, by golly."

"I am so glad for you, Pate. I really am." She realized she sounded a little wistful and tried to pick her tone up.

"Lacey, hon, all things work for the best, just like the Good Book says. I'm tellin' you that this is all gonna work out for your good, too—better than you imagine."

"I hope so." Then, more positively, "I'm countin' on it."

"Well, I know Cooper can be a mite disagreeable, and this is all an upset to your plans. But I know, too, that Cooper will see you and the children safely to Pine Grove. Don't you worry. I've known Cooper for nigh on to twenty years now, since his first years drivin'. He's a good reliable driver. A good *man*."

"I know you wouldn't have asked him to drive us if you didn't believe he'd take care of us."

"No, I wouldn't have. Now, honey, you need to see your folks and get things all patched up there, and well, Cooper needs your company on this trip. Holidays are a mighty lonesome time for him."

Lacey thought that Cooper didn't seem like the type of man to want, much less need, anyone, but she said, "We'll all be just fine, Pate. And I'll telephone you just as soon as we get back."

They wished each other Merry Christmas and hung up.

Then, standing there with her hand still on the receiver, Lacey realized she had missed the chance to ask Cooper's full name.

Their duplex apartment dated from the fifties, and the years could be counted by the thick layers of paint. There was a living room, kitchen, and two bedrooms, and in order that her children could each have their own, Lacey slept on the pullout sofa bed in the living room.

She pulled out the bed in the dimly lit room and placed the traveling bags on it, throwing a few things in them that she'd bought that evening. One hand on her hip and the other raking through her hair, she looked at the worn bags, the worn quilt, the shadows on the worn walls. Not at all like the warm, graceful home where she had grown up.

Her parents' house was two-story brick, with a small rounded entry porch. A banker's house, Lacey and her sister Beth used to joke. Their father had been a banker, a loan officer. On more than one occasion his refusal of a loan request had proven embarrassing for his daughters, who received the punishing resentment from the children of the parents who had been denied. Lacey and

Beth heard the rumors about their father being a hard man, an "old miser" and an "old skinflint."

Funny, Lacey thought now in remembering, how much the criticism had overshadowed in her mind the good parts of her father, who had also been well respected. He had been the one the school board called when the budget was in crisis, the one everyone leaned on during the various crises experienced by many of their extended family of aunts and uncles, even neighbors.

But in her impressionable teen years her father and the house they lived in had been too stuffy for Lacey, and very often the look of prosperity had embarrassed her. As a teenager, something within her had not allowed her to fit in with those who lived as she did, and because of the way she lived, she did not fit in with those who had less, either. She never had felt she fit in anywhere, and she had blamed her parents.

With the passage of years, she saw her life with clarity. And her heart longed for both her family and the old house, especially as her mother would decorate for the holidays—the shiny green leaves and red berries of holly gleaming from the mantel and polished tabletops, and the pungent smell of pine wafting through the house from the great, glittering tree in the foyer.

Her father had always seemed to mellow at Christmastime. He encouraged holiday festivities and parties, inviting in family and neighbors, even some he preferred to ignore for the rest of the year. He would take Lacey and Beth out to a friend's land and be uncharacteristically patient while they tramped for acres, searching for just the right tree. Then he would chop it down and haul it back to the house atop their big gleaming Chevy station wagon. It had been their father who had always set the angel atop the tree.

"He couldn't straighten enough to get the angel on top this year," Beth had said. *"He's getting old."*

"Has he said my name?"

"No…but he will, if you come home."

With a sigh, Lacey sank down on the edge of the pull-out bed. After a moment, she picked up the picture album she had assembled as her parents' gift: a photo album chronicling the young lives of their grandchildren. The years the grandparents had missed, and which Lacey hoped could be made up with time and forgiveness.

Slowly, in the yellow glow of the table lamp, she

turned the album pages. The first pictures were of Jon when he'd been only weeks old.

She touched her fingertips to the glossy photograph, and her mind sped back in time.

She had been barely nineteen.

"You have to tell them."

"I know."

Leaving Beth to listen from the stairway, Lacey entered the living room. "Mom...Dad?"

Her parents sat opposite each other in front of the fireplace. Her mother looked up from studying a cookbook, and her father said, "Hmm?" without putting down his newspaper.

"I have something to tell you... I'm pregnant."

Her mother had been shocked and confused. "How could you...when did you...I've told you what can happen." She reached her arms out toward Lacey, but did not move from her chair. She was too inhibited by her husband, who was on his feet and in a rage.

"Well, who is it? Do you know?"

His accusation had cut to the bone. "Of course I know, Daddy. It's Shawn." Seeing the fury in her father's face, she could not speak further.

Her father had never liked Shawn, because he didn't go to college.

"What will people say?" said her mother, her eyes wet with tears and shame. "How will we show our faces in church now?"

Their town was small, provincial, and their world was like this, too.

Her father said, "Girl, you know better. You know what sin is. You've put this family down."

She could not believe the scorn and anger he shot toward her.

Her parents insisted she give the baby up for adoption.

She refused. "I love my baby." She pressed a hand to her belly. "I'm going to have your grandchild," she told them.

But her mother, who kept crying, said, "What future will you have?"

And her father said, "You give the baby up for adoption, or you get out." He kept to this stance for the next two days, even when her mother and Beth pleaded with him.

Finally Lacey left, screaming over her shoulder at him, "You are a mean, hateful man, and I don't want my baby around you. I'll never come back."

There had been nowhere to go, of course, but to Shawn, who, to his credit, agreed without a grumble to marry her. The ceremony took place in the justice's office at the courthouse, after Lacey had taken care of all the necessary details, even to pointing out the places for Shawn to sign on each of the forms.

She stood before the justice holding flowers that she had purchased herself, while Shawn stood beside her in a borrowed suit that was much too large. Their two witnesses were her sister Beth and Shawn's best friend, Lloyd, who wore a worn leather biker jacket. They started out like a million other young couples in the world—broke, and with a family on the way.

Shawn displayed promise when he immediately enlisted, somehow managing to get himself into the air force as a mechanic, which gave him not only a good steady job but also a bit of schooling, and enabled Lacey to have medical care for her pregnancy.

Almost a month overdue, alone on a military base far from home, because Shawn was off with the air force, she produced Jon, a big bouncing boy.

Holding her new son in her arms, she telephoned home.

"Lacey?" There was some warmth in her mother's voice.

"I wanted to tell you that I had a boy. I've named him Jon."

"A boy…oh, my, Lacey, honey…"

They talked a little bit, and her mother cried. She promised to speak with Lacey's father.

But while their conversation gave Lacey some hope of reconciliation, the connection left unsatisfactory feelings of doubt and disappointment in that her mother did not immediately get on a bus to come help with the baby.

And when the days and nights passed in which Lacey walked the floor with her new infant all alone, without a mother's guiding hand, and without any further word from either parent, disappointment solidified into resentment.

"Mom just can't," said Beth, who called a number of times. "She can't help it, Lacey. It just isn't in her to go against Daddy. You can't blame her for not being what we want her to be."

Beth, the oldest, came to that understanding far earlier than Lacey, who would in the passing years come to comprehension, but would have difficulty getting over the hurt of the betrayal. She threw herself into being the best, most perfect mother possible to her son, and then to her daughter. She vowed never to betray them in abandonment, the way she felt her parents had betrayed her. She sought to heal her own heartache by giving her children the nurturing love that she herself craved.

Shawn, however, did not so readily take up with being a father. His early display of promise turned out to be the only bit he would show toward family responsibility. He often went absent from home, and without explanation, and on several occasions he went absent from the air force, too. After two years, the air force gave up on him, but Lacey didn't know anything else to do but to keep holding on.

One day, six months after Anna had been born, she came home to find Shawn packing.

"I just can't do it anymore, Lacey. I'm sorry."

She thought but did not say, *"You never did do it,"* and then set about helping him to pack. She had been alone, really, since leaving her parents, thus she was not afraid of being alone physically.

After Shawn left, Lacey had sat on the front stoop, feeling relieved that taking care of him was over. Holding Anna and watching Jon play in the yard, she began to realize that leaving home and everything she had dealt with since had given her something—it had given her some unexplainable faith in God, and this brought faith in herself. She would manage. She would get through.

Coming slowly back to the present, Lacey found herself gazing at the picture of Anna on her most recent birthday. She smiled sadly, thinking of Shawn and all that he missed by not being able to give of himself. She thought of her parents, too, and all they had missed by not being able to give of themselves.

She couldn't help Shawn, but she could help her parents, and herself and the children. She could give her parents a chance.

Closing the photo album, she went once more to the phone on the wall in the kitchen and dialed Beth's number.

"I just need to touch base…there's been a change in plans." She gripped the receiver as she told her sister about the switch in circumstances. "You're sure you shouldn't tell Daddy about us? I would just hate to have the kids experience him turnin' us away."

"He won't turn you away…not when he sees you

standin' there." Then, "Come home, Lacey. I miss you."

"I miss you, too. We'll be there."

She brought out the wrapping paper and ribbon, poured another cup of coffee and turned on the little portable radio. It took a bit of adjusting the knob to get a station in without too much static—country music interspersed with carols.

Humming along, she wrapped the photo album and the last few presents on the kitchen table. The very last of these was one she'd bought Cooper—she gazed at the burnished metal buckle nested in its small box. It was cast with images of trucking: a smoking tractor-trailer rig, exaggerated tires and highway signs.

Perhaps he would think it a cheap gift, which it was. It had been cut to half price. And giving such a personal gift to a man whose full name she didn't even know seemed awfully silly. No doubt she would feel odd when she gave it, and he would feel odd taking it.

But it was a token of appreciation. She needed to express that, she thought emphatically, as she cut the elf-paper to wrap it and decorated it with her own brand of ribbon magic, until it looked like some sort of wild, colorful explosion.

While she worked, she thought that though she treasured the presents she received—nonsensical things made by childish but dear hands—she sometimes longed for a special present from a man in her life.

She found herself pulling everything out of her drawers and closet, despairing over the lack of suitable outfits. All her clothes seemed so worn and out of date. And suddenly looking her best, not only when she arrived on her parents' doorstep but during the trip, was very important.

She did have one pair of fairly new blue jeans—designer ones bought on sale—and there was the mauve sweater that brought out her skin tone. They would do for the first day. And it wasn't too much trouble to roll her hair after washing it. That would hold up for two days. Possibly painted nails would last all the way there. Her mother had always said a little color on the nails made a woman's hands look more feminine. Her mother would be pleased if Lacey turned up looking her best.

It was after one o'clock before she got to sleep, and

she didn't sleep much, tossing and turning, the rollers poking into her scalp no matter what position she tried.

But the next morning her hair looked great. And she was so keyed up, her face appeared vibrant instead of worn out. She decided she looked pretty good in her jeans, too, and her efforts served to make her feel confident about the trip ahead.

As she applied a bit of lipstick, she thought that maybe yesterday had been simply a bad one for Cooper, making him abnormally grumpy. Maybe today he would welcome them, even be glad to have their company.

"It's a thought," she murmured to the skeptical-looking image in the mirror.

Surprise

Lacey parked out of the way at Gerald's lot and tucked the key beneath the mat—not that anyone was likely to steal the car—and that way Jolene could start it a few times to keep the battery up and everything lubricated. Lacey was afraid that if left to sit for ten whole days, the car might never start again.

"Middle of the damn…darn night," Jon grumbled.

Lacey silently agreed as she settled the children in a front booth, where she could watch for Cooper's arrival through the big window. With the night's blackness broken only by the building's silvery outside lights, the window reflected her family's faces.

Her own image startled her. When had she become a full woman? A mother? And was that really her with the nice curly hair? Was that woman's figure—shapely and feminine—really hers?

She didn't feel like that inside. Inside she felt quivery and sort of small and uncertain, although she was very careful to hide these emotions from her children.

Well, she'd gone too far to back out now, she thought, digging into her tote bag for a tissue for Anna.

"Order anything you want, kids," she told them when Paloma, who was working the early shift, came over. "We have over half an hour."

"It's too early to eat," Jon said.

"Try."

"Three days until Christmas," Anna piped up out of the blue, giving a bright smile and telling Paloma she wanted Cheerios.

For the next twenty-five minutes, Lacey's heartbeat gradually picked up tempo and her insides began to quiver more than ever before as her mind raced from worry about traveling with Cooper to worry about her father's possible angry reaction. When Jon, who'd been craning his neck to peer out the window, said, "Did you say Cooper's truck was red?" she almost jumped out of her seat.

"Maroon," she answered.

And there it was, a big, shiny, top-of-the-line Kenworth truck pulling a silver trailer, rolling to a stop several yards away. It gleamed in the fluorescent lighting.

A distinctly sinking feeling claimed her when her gaze fell to the Christmas lights draped across the Kenworth's grill. In merry greens, reds and yellows, the lights crudely spelled out: *Bah Humbug.*

She stared at them for approximately thirty seconds. Yes, that's what they said.

She grasped at the idea that maybe it wasn't Cooper. Plenty of drivers drove such trucks. Maybe it was someone else.

Then a figure dressed in a thick vest, shoulders hunched against the cold, with a black Stetson on his head, strode around the front of the truck toward the restaurant.

It was Cooper.

Lacey looked at her children. Jon's eyebrows went up in silent question.

"It's Cooper," she said.

"Ba…ba…hum…?" Anna's eyebrows were furrowed as she tried to read.

Jon filled in. "Bah Humbug—like old Scrooge." Then he muttered, "I get this funny feeling…" He stopped at Lacey's sharp look.

"Here, Anna, let's get your coat on," Lacey said, casting both children a bright smile. "It's time to go."

Without looking, she mentally pictured Cooper striding into the restaurant. She knew exactly when he entered. She felt a cold breeze—and his gaze. She looked up and across the room.

Cooper was frowning—in fact, his expression was thunderous—as he approached. In the process of buttoning Anna's coat, Lacey's fingers stilled. She could do no more than stare at him and wonder what she'd done, because it was obvious he was furious with her.

Cooper knew it was Pate's fault, but Pate wasn't here, and Lacey was. And she should have said something about the kids yesterday.

"Good morning," she said to him now.

He looked at her, and then he turned his gaze to the two pint-size kids. Then he looked back at her again.

She was saying, "I'd like you to meet my children, Cooper," her voice polite and soft, just as if nothing was wrong. "This is Jon…" she touched the boy's shoulder, "…and this is Anna."

"Pate didn't say anything about kids," Cooper managed to get out in a low voice. *He wanted out of this, and he intended to get out. He wasn't spending three days in the cab of his truck with two wet-nosed kids.*

"You didn't…" Her green eyes searched his. "Pate didn't tell you I had two children—that he was taking all of us to Pine Grove?"

"No, ma'am, he did not. He neglected that fact. And so did you yesterday." So now she would apologize, and the trip would be off.

"Well, I'm sorry…"

She looked confused and apologetic. And her eyes were extremely dark against the paleness of her face. A shaft of disappointment touched Cooper. Why did she have to go and have kids? He'd almost been thinking it would be nice to drive east with her, that having her along might make the stretch ahead seem shorter.

A stupid thought that had been.

Just then she said, "I had no idea. I simply assumed

you knew. Pate's note said it was all arranged, and last night when I spoke to him, he didn't say there could be any problem."

She seemed to have grown taller or something. She was looking him right in the eye.

"No, I guess he didn't," Cooper allowed, his gaze dropping again to the children in front of him.

One was a little girl, short straight brown hair and wide brown eyes and a heart-shaped face. She clung to her mother's leg and regarded Cooper as she would a horned devil. The boy was about ten, maybe eleven, with tousled light brown hair and eyes, and a body stance that indicated he knew all there was to know in this world.

"Well," Lacey said, "as I said before, these are my children, Jon and Anna." She rested her hand atop the little girl's head and smiled at Cooper. "Kids, this is Mr.—this is Cooper, who's generously agreed to take Pate's place and drive us to Pine Grove. Isn't that nice of him?"

Cooper stared at her. He swallowed as he stared into her clear eyes, which held nothing but expectation.

How had she done it? One minute she had looked

hesitant, vague and on the verge of running, and the next she was acting as if everything was going perfectly smoothly, like a blacktop highway snaking off into the prairie.

What could he say?

"Come on. We got three days to get there, and I'd as soon make it in two."

He pivoted and strode toward the restaurant doors, followed by the sound of "Jingle Bells" that some jerk had punched into the jukebox, regardless of it being five in the morning.

Bah humbug!

Three days in the cab of his rig with a woman and two wet-nosed kids. Wasn't that just fine and dandy?

A *beautiful* woman and two wet-nosed kids, he thought as he paused at the truck's passenger door and turned to watch the gal and kids approach. He tried to wiggle from the thought, but it stuck fast as he watched them approach. She carried a bulging suitcase in each hand, and another bag hung from her shoulder, but she walked straight and with firm steps. The cold breeze blew her hair back from her face; small gold hoop earrings caught the fluorescent lights.

"Five bags aren't gonna fit," he told her, gesturing toward the bags the children also carried.

"This is a tote bag," she said, indicating the large one hanging from her shoulder. "And Pate said we could bring four suitcases."

Cooper was rewarded by the slight quaver in her voice and the uncertainty that glimmered momentarily in her eyes.

"I ain't Pate."

"You want me to leave one behind? Where should I leave it?"

"Here's fine with me." He felt foolish at his words, and more angry because of the feeling.

She stared at him. "We need all four bags—and everything in this tote. There *are* three of us."

"Rearrange things. There isn't room."

A movement drew his gaze, and Cooper glanced down to see the little girl gaping at him. Her face began to squinch up, and her lips to tremble. Regret seemed to slip up and get him from behind.

"Okay, fine!" the gal yelled at him and plunked down the two bulging bags. The next instant she had knelt down, unzipped one of them and gone to jerking clothes from it. A blue sweatshirt went flying to the pavement. "I can do without this...or this..."

A flutter of white followed the sweatshirt, then several frilly pink things that resembled a nightgown and underwear, giving Cooper an uncomfortable feeling in the pit of his stomach. Suddenly he was aware of the cold and of several curious faces peering through the restaurant windows.

He knelt and quickly grabbed the scattered clothes, catching a pair of panties that came sailing his way.

"All right!" He thrust the clothes at her. "Put these back in there, and let's get goin'. At this rate it's gonna be six before we get out of here."

Adjusting his hat low on his brow, he strode around the front of the truck, leaving the gal and her kids to get inside as best they could.

Heading East

Watching Cooper disappear around the front of the big truck, Lacey contemplated words too ugly to speak. She was embarrassed by her actions, furious with his, and she didn't know what to do about the entire situation.

"I don't like him, Mama," Anna said, slipping an arm around Lacey's leg.

"You sure you still want to do this, Mom?" Jon asked.

Lacey looked at him. "Oh, yes," she responded.

Turning from her son's gaze, she grabbed hold of a handle and hoisted herself up into the vibrating truck.

Jon handed up each bag, which she piled on and between the seats. Then she helped the children up and peered in the rear of the truck cab with widening eyes.

In all her years of working at the truck stop, watching the rigs come and go, Lacey had never been inside one. She'd heard of the renowned Kenworth truck, but her imagination hadn't done it justice.

Though the big engine ran, it sent only a gentle, even pleasant rumble into the truck cab itself, which was cozy, warm. The two high-backed seats were upholstered in thick gray velour and resembled living-room recliners, complete with armrests. Tufted gray vinyl lined the door panels and roof, and thick gunmetal-gray carpeting covered the floor.

In the center, behind the chairs, was the opening to the sleeping compartment.

"Man-o-man," said Jon, who could stand in the compartment and move about easily.

Lacey, bending slightly, paused to stare at the padded vinyl lining the walls and ceiling, and the bed that seemed queen-size at least, and the luxurious blue bedspread.

"There's a TV!" Jon exclaimed, drawing Lacey's gaze to the small portable on the shelf. Color, no less. There were also speakers in the wall, indicating a stereo system somewhere.

Lacey opened what she thought to be a cabinet and found a refrigerator instead. Straightening, she came face-to-face with a microwave oven. In a narrow closet hung several pairs of jeans and numerous shirts, a pair of shiny boots sitting beneath them.

"Where's the shower?" she quipped to Cooper, who had just entered the rig.

His answer was a low grunt. He sat in his seat behind the wheel, apparently engrossed in checking the numerous gauges on the dash, recording things in some sort of log, and generally acting as if he were alone in the rig, as no doubt he wished to be.

Lacey squeezed three of their bags into a large, only partially filled cabinet beneath the bed. She was standing in the narrow compartment opening, debating what to do with the fourth bag, when Cooper rose up beside her.

"Haven't gotten the shower installed yet," he said.

She couldn't tell if he was joking or not.

"All set?" he asked.

With a suddenness, she became aware of the scent of his sweet-musky after-shave. She didn't want to notice it. And then he turned to look at her, his face, lit by the golden glow of the interior lights, only inches away.

"I don't know where to put this bag," Lacey had to admit.

His eyes were deep and dark, his eyelashes long, his mustache slightly bristly, and his hair quite wavy, all of which in one instant she noticed and thought she should not.

His arm came around in front of her, causing her to pull back and suck in, as he tossed his hat onto a hook above the television. Then, without a word, Cooper squeezed past her, his thighs rubbing hers, his belt buckle pressing her arm. Lacey felt flustered. She was suddenly aware of being a woman, which brought with it the disturbing awareness that Cooper was very much a man.

She watched him bend at the knee in order to fit into the compartment and open a cabinet above the end of the bed. He pulled out two blankets, tossed them beside Anna and Jon, sitting on the bed, grabbed the bag from Lacey and stuffed it in the cabinet, shutting it with a hard snap.

He looked at her, and she looked at him.

Realizing she was in his way, she searched for somewhere to go. The only place was the passenger seat. She sat down.

Cooper slipped into the driver's chair, flipped switches and turned on the headlights.

Anna came quietly to wiggle onto Lacey's lap. Lacey held her close, rubbing her cheek on Anna's hair. She worried if she had made a huge mistake in choosing to continue with her trip. It had been pride, of course, that had taken hold in the parking lot. But now she wondered whether it could possibly harm her children to take this trip with a man who so obviously didn't want them around.

One worry in, all the others multiplied. What if she could not handle her temper with this most disagreeable man? What if, at the trip's end, her father rejected them, too?

"Can I watch the television, Mr. Cooper?" Jon called from the back.

Lacey had to smile. Obviously her son was not bothered by Cooper's rudeness. But then, Jon could generally return as good as he got. The Lord had blessed him with resilience.

"Yeah," Cooper said. Then, his hand on the

gearshift, he looked at Lacey and said, "She can't stay here. It's not safe."

Anna gripped Lacey and wasn't about to let go.

"I'll get in the back with her."

Cooper nodded and turned his attention to getting underway. As Lacey cleared the pass-through, Cooper jerked a curtain across the opening, enclosing her and the children in the cozy confines of the sleeper—and himself up front, alone.

The truck gave a gentle jolt of forward motion, and they were off. Lacey gratefully stretched out beside Anna beneath the blankets. She was exhausted and quite chilled.

Jon figured out how to work the television in the manner of modern children who can automatically work any electronic equipment, and Lacey, drowsy, marveled. Then Jon propped himself against her feet, avidly watching a cartoon show, the television providing the only light in the compartment. Lacey listened to the rumble of the engine and felt the rhythmic motion of the vehicle. It was a comfort to have both children physically touching her.

"It's like being rocked," Anna whispered, her eyes filled with wonder.

"Mmm…" Lacey hugged her daughter closer, feeling suddenly a raw spot in her heart. She mused over the idea of spending the entire trip in the sleeping compartment. Surely that would make Mr. Delightful happy. How in the world could Pate think Cooper needed company?

Cooper shifted gears, feeling the big Kenworth easily gain speed. The headlights illuminated the highway ahead. There was a surprising amount of traffic for so early in the morning. People trying to get home for the holidays, he thought, half bitterly, half wistfully.

The road passed beneath the rig at seventy miles an hour. He glanced at the speedometer and increased speed, then eased up, letting the speed drop back again. Three days stretched ahead of him before he dropped his load—Pate's load—up in D.C. He could make it in much less than three if he drove as he usually did. But with the woman and two kids, he probably wouldn't.

He glanced in the mirror, looking at the curtains of the sleeper. He wondered what the gal was doing back there. In his bed.

He wondered what had happened to her husband. Pate had just said that she was on her own, something

Cooper had surmised after many meals at Gerald's, but now he wondered if he had simply jumped to a conclusion. And he had been more preoccupied with how to get around Pate's request than asking a lot of questions about the woman.

Chances were she was divorced. Most were. She might be a widow. Funny how he never really had heard much about her despite all the times he'd stopped at Gerald's. He wasn't so much of a talker, though, and did not listen much to gossip.

Maybe her husband was in prison. He had met a couple of waitresses whose husbands were in prison. Maybe her husband had run off, which happened a lot. Or maybe she ran around. She didn't seem the type, but in his experience, very often people weren't at all what they seemed. Especially women.

His spirit seemed to slide downward quite suddenly. Was she going to spend the entire trip back there in the sleeper? Now that she was here, the least she could do was get up front and fill his coffee cup from his Thermos.

In a quick motion, he reached over and turned up the volume on the radio. A good Randy Travis country tune floated out, and he gave thanks that it did not have a hint of Christmas in it.

The sky began to glow with morning. Cooper shifted in his seat and took note of the steering wheel in his hands and the smooth rumble of the truck pushing through the wind and rolling over the road. The experience never failed to give him a boost.

A fool in a red Corvette pulled dangerously close in front of him, and he let up on the accelerator. The fact of his passengers suddenly seemed to sit on his shoulders. He thought that many companies had the right idea by ruling out passengers altogether. He should have made that rule for himself. He would from now on. Next time someone requested he take passengers, he would say, "No, my company doesn't allow it."

The little girl's expression that morning came across his mind. Was he really so much of a monster? He leaned over and checked his image in the mirror.

He supposed he did look pretty rough. He rubbed a hand over his hair, which was beginning to gray and could use cutting. He was thirty-eight years old, single for most of those years, no kids, and he didn't much like them, either. Children reminded him of

Martians, a little species with customs and language all their own.

He jerked his mind from the dreary thoughts and began to hum along with the radio. The cab didn't seem so empty then. But he didn't want to be heard, so he kept the humming faint.

Minutes later, the dividing curtain was pushed open. The humming died in his throat as he met the gal's gaze in the rearview mirror.

He averted his gaze to the side mirror, but not before he saw her smile. She had a rare kind of smile. It lit up her entire face.

He wanted to smile in return, only he didn't. That would be stupid. He didn't want her to get the idea she was welcome or anything.

But, he thought, catching sight of her as she slipped into the passenger seat, he had to admit to himself that he didn't mind looking at her. Not at all.

He noticed her move the armrests up and down, then give a little bounce, testing the seat like a kid.

Stretching over, he moved the lever to activate the air cushion. She jumped, and her eyes widened.

"The air," he said, quickly returning his hand to the wheel, "for the seat." *What did she think—that he was trying to cop a feel?*

He returned his strict attention to the road ahead. It felt odd to have her beside him. He had never had a woman in his rig, had always purposefully avoided it.

Lacey didn't realize she was studying Cooper until he glanced over at her. Self-conscious, she jerked her head to look out the side window and folded her hands in her lap. Perfectly composed. Of course she was. And she didn't care what Cooper thought of her.

It was cozy in the cab. The change in the seat when he'd moved that lever had surprised her. And now it was like an easy chair at home, though it rocked a bit more. She loved the lordly height of the truck the very best. They passed a Toyota, and she looked down to see the driver's knees, which seemed an intimate observation.

The eastern horizon stretched orange, while faint stars still shone above. The sparse woods and dry land they passed showed signs of heavy frost.

"Looks like a sunny day," Lacey commented. She loved sunny mornings.

"Radio says clouds ahead," Cooper said.

"Oh."

Then she spied a slowly pumping oil well draped with colorful Christmas lights. "Look! Aren't they pretty?" she said, before she thought. She glanced at Cooper, who, with absolutely no appreciation at all, gave a grunt and kept his eyes on the road.

A man of few words, Lacey thought, feeling self-conscious and childish—and irritable because of it.

He pushed in the lighter, pulled a cigarette from his shirt pocket and tucked it between his lips. *Oh, dear.* It was his truck, after all. And for all the attention he paid her, Lacey noted, she might as well not be there.

Well, there was no reason why she should receive his attention, she told herself, thinking of the hours and hours ahead of them. Jolene had said Cooper had a softer side, and Pate had said Cooper needed people at this time of year. Maybe he was just sour and distant because he was shy. She could try harder to extend a friendly hand.

"What's a Jacob's Brake?" she asked.

Cooper gave her a lazy glance. "What?"

"That." She pointed to the switch. "What sort of brake is that?"

"A brake is all," he said. "I got a lot of wheels to stop."
He jerked his thumb back toward the trailer.

Obviously it was something he felt that she, a mere
woman, wouldn't understand.

She took a deep breath and pushed away her irrita-
tion. "I had no idea these trucks were like this," she said
brightly. "So luxurious. It's really a work of art."

He grunted around his cigarette.

Lacey refused to give up. There'd been few people in
all her life she couldn't relate to, make friends with. All
it took was being friendly first, and that didn't cost much.

She continued to ask questions, and he answered—
with one- and two-word sentences, or the now familiar
grunt. He was hauling computer printers, Pate's payload. He'd known Pate for twenty years. He lived not
far from Pate in Santa Fe. Yes, he liked Santa Fe, as
much as anywhere, at least. When he showed no incli-
nation to continue polite conversation, Lacey fell to silently staring out the window.

For some unfathomable reason, she wanted to
smack him.

"Would you pour me some coffee?"

Cooper's voice startled her. He handed her the cup

from the nearby holder. "The Thermos is right behind my seat," he said.

"Oh…sure!" She was pleased that he'd asked her to do something. At least he'd spoken words she had not pried out of him.

She filled his cup with hot coffee, and automatically stirred in sugar from the packets she had seen tucked into the dash. "One sugar, right?" she said, handing the cup to him with a smile.

"Yeah…thanks," he said, without a smile of his own, and seeming to pull back down his shield.

The only sounds in the cab for the next fifteen minutes were the engine's low rumble and music from the radio. When there came a loud crackling static and a man's voice calling out, "Hey, snappy maroon Kenworth," Lacey jumped.

"Got your ears on, Kenworth?" came the call again.

Cooper reached up and got the CB radio microphone. "You got the Solitary Man."

Lacey thought he had named himself aptly. She listened as he exchanged information with the unseen driver, who was heading west, about conditions on the interstate. Lacey heard some terms she understood and some that baffled her. Cooper said he had not seen or heard of the "bear in the air," a police plane, that the other driver had heard of, and both men concluded it was safe for "pedal to the metal." Then Cooper said, "Five bye-bye," and hung up the microphone.

Lacey stared at him. "Do you know him—Mr. Zoo Keeper?" That was what the other driver had called himself.

Cooper slid his gaze to her. "Just another trucker, is all."

She looked at the road ahead and thought how he had actually carried on a friendly conversation with a total stranger. Something he apparently didn't want to do with her.

Five minutes later, Jon poked a bright face around the curtain. "I'm hungry, Mom."

Cooper gave his familiar grunt, and Lacey dug into her tote bag, pulling out a snack cake and handing it to her son.

"You know the danger of cancer is about tripled for passive smokers," Jon said, waving at Cooper's cigarette smoke.

"Then sit in the back so you won't suffer," Cooper drawled.

Lacey, turning her gaze out the window, vowed to curtail her son's television news watching.

Lord, how she hated discord in any form. This thought came with a flow of memories of her father, and then, unbidden, scenes from her life, causing an uncomfortable realization that she didn't simply hate discord, she ran from it at every turn. She did everything she could to get along, and maybe this wasn't such a good thing. Yet—she glanced at Cooper—she could not recall ever being in such close contact with a person who plain didn't like her. It hurt and confused her.

"Mama, I have to go to the bathroom," Anna's young voice squeaked as she poked a sleepy-eyed face beside Jon's.

Cooper looked at Lacey as if he wanted to scream. Very quietly he said, "There's a rest stop up the road, about ten minutes."

"That will be fine." She gave a pleasant smile.

A little past nine o'clock, after the third time the kids said they were hungry, Lacey said to him, "I'm sure Mr. Cooper is about ready to stop for breakfast."

"Oh, yeah," he told her.

It so happened that a truck stop he regularly frequented was another mile up the road. He pulled in and over to refuel, since he was stopping.

Lacey and her kids went on ahead to the restaurant, while he lagged behind to give his brakes a thorough inspection. They'd been performing okay, but he had a sense of unease. Having passengers was putting him on edge, he thought.

The uncomfortable thought came across his mind that he had gotten set in his ways. That he was looking close at forty. Where had his life gone? What did he have to show for any of it?

He pushed the thoughts aside and paid attention to checking out the truck. Finding nothing amiss, he headed for the building, working his shoulders and forcing relaxation, thinking that nothing in his deal with Pate said he had to do anything but give these people a ride. He didn't have to eat with them.

He paid for his fuel, then headed for the restaurant, his appetite kindled by the aroma of strong coffee and frying sausage.

The trucker store was strategically placed in the path of the restaurant entryway. A display of the latest in compact disc players for vehicles drew Cooper's attention. He paused to look at one.

"Pretty slick machine," came a voice from beside him. "Maybe Santa will leave one in your stocking."

Recognizing the smart tone of voice, Cooper slowly turned his head to see the kid, Jon, at his elbow. The boy had slicked his light brown hair back from his face and had his hands stuffed into his fashionably baggy denims.

"Listen, kid," Cooper said, "you have to work for what you want in this life. There's no free ride. I learned it by the age of five—there is no Santa Claus."

The boy's easy grin seemed to melt and slide right off his face. He turned his head, and Cooper followed the boy's gaze. A sinking feeling came over him as he spotted the red coat. The little girl, Anna, stood on the other side of the boy. She looked up at Cooper, her lower lip trembling.

"Anna...Jon." Lacey appeared from the nearby ladies' room doorway. Her eyes moved quickly from the children to Cooper and back again. The little girl ran to clutch her mother around the leg.

Cooper looked at the mother and her little girl, who was again regarding him as if he had horns.

He said, "Better get some breakfast, 'cause I'm leavin' here in thirty-five minutes," and made an immediate exit toward the dining room.

Puzzled, Lacey watched Cooper stride away. She looked down at Anna.

"Mama," Anna said, her lower lip trembling and eyes tearing, "he said there's no Santa Claus."

Uh-oh. "I'm sure he didn't mean exactly that, Anna."

"He said it," Anna announced logically.

"Aw, Anna," Jon said, "you know some people like to say stuff like that. Cooper, he don't know. He's just like that Scrooge guy in the movie we saw. He can't enjoy Christmas so he'd just as soon spoil it. Now come on— I'm starved."

Believing in Santa

Lacey sent her son a grateful look. She was for the moment saved, but as they ate, Anna pressed her again about Santa Claus. "How does he get all over the world in one night, Mama? Mia says that isn't possible," she said, quoting a school friend.

"Well, sweetheart, Santa Claus is a special man," Lacey said, feeling she was digging her hole deeper and deeper, but she wanted Anna to have the fairy tale as long as possible. "He is magic…and he doesn't ever get tired." Oh, dear, Anna was regarding her with her big brown eyes.

"Well, for one thing," Jon said, "Santa don't go…"

"*Doesn't* go," Lacey interjected automatically, her attention on Cooper, who had gone to sit at the counter. Like a child, she thought. Although what he did was no concern of hers. She just found it awkward to see him sitting across the room. Here they were, traveling in the same vehicle, but they weren't friendly enough to eat together.

"…doesn't go to all the people of the world. Christmas came from Jesus's birth, you know, and a lot of people don't believe in Jesus…don't even know nothin' about Christmas."

"They don't?" Anna frowned, turning this piece of information over. "They don't know about Christmas?"

"Well, I guess most ever'body knows, but they don't celebrate it. You got your Jewish people, and your Islamic people, and the Buddhists—none of them celebrate Christmas."

"Really, Mama?"

"Yes, honey." Lacey was thinking how she wasn't friendly enough with Cooper to even ask his full name. Did they have to be friends for her to ask that?

"They don't get presents?" Anna's voice trembled.

"Oh, they have their own celebration times with presents," Jon said quickly. "They have people and things to celebrate, too. But they don't have Santa, so the most he has to cover is Europe, and that's not too big, and North and South America, and these spotty places in the rest of the world."

"Does he only go to those children who believe in Jesus?" Anna clearly had a new concern.

"Well, yes, mostly," Jon answered, although he did see trouble. "But like I said, it is okay, because the other children, they have special people of their own and special times to get presents. They get lots of presents, just not from Santa Claus."

Anna still looked a little worried over the matter.

"Anna, here, blow your nose." She should tell Anna the truth. Finding out her mother lied to her would likely cause Anna to question everything Lacey said. Probably that was where everyone's trouble started.

This entire trip was not going to work, she thought, having a sinking moment. The situation wasn't fair to the children, nor to Cooper. She did not think she could remain all sweetness and light for the remainder of the trip, not to mention coming back. "Finish your milk," she said to both children.

After a minute, Anna said, "But how does Santa get to all the people in all the countries? I just don't see—"

"The time difference," Jon put in, his mouth full of food.

"Jon, don't bolt your food. We have time to eat." Lacey wasn't about to have her son choke just to please Solitary-Man-Cooper.

"You see," Jon continued, his voice taking on the quality it did when he was gearing up for a long-winded explanation, which he made as he continued to shovel food into his mouth, "it's the time difference. When it is Christmas Day here, it has already been Christmas Day over in France, so Santa's already been there. See, the world turns this way…" He illustrated the turning with his glass of milk. "And Santa's going this way, which gives him three days to complete his job."

Anna stared at him. "It's gonna take us three days to get to our grandma's. Will Santa miss us?"

"No," said Jon with impatience. "Santa don— doesn't miss anybody. He's got electronic devices that tell him everything. And we're goin' by truck, but Santa has this super high-velocity sled, and then there are sta-tions all over, where he stops for the presents and to re-fuel…you know, like the space station. And Santa moves sort of like the speed of light, like those stealth airplanes, so fast that you can only see him once in a while when he slows down at a house." Jon was getting into this very much.

"The weather man sees him on radar."

"Yeah, radar can see him…but only sometimes."

"But what about when he stops at houses to put the stuff under the tree and eat his cookies?" Anna's eyebrows came together.

"Some people see him then, but he's still pretty fast."

Lacey saw Cooper rising from his stool. He glanced over at them.

"Come on, children."

Jon saw Cooper leaving and hurried after him, tossing over his shoulder to Lacey, "I'll go see if I can help him with anything."

Digging into her purse for a tip for the waitress, Lacey started to call him back, but then shut her mouth. Her son needed an outlet for his boundless energy, which was just going to grow as the day went along.

"Mama, why is Cooper so grumpy?" Anna asked.

Lacey, buttoning her daughter's coat, stopped and looked into her deep brown eyes. "I'm not certain, honey. A lot of times a person gets like that from sad things that have happened in their life."

"Maybe he doesn't believe in Santa Claus because Santa doesn't bring him anything—because he's too grumpy all the time."

"Oh, sweetie, Santa brings everyone presents. Even grumpy people. He loves everyone…but maybe Cooper can't see the presents, so he doesn't accept them." She took Anna's hand.

"That's one of those things I'll understand when I'm older, right?" Anna said very seriously.

They had traveled thirty minutes down the road and the children were taking a nap when Lacey finally worked up enough courage to tell Cooper that she intended for her and the children to make the return trip by bus. She would borrow the money from Beth. She could even borrow from her father, providing her father was speaking to them. She would do something, anything, but she could not ride back with him. She even toyed with the idea of having him let them off in Oklahoma City, at the bus station. But this presented the problem of finding the bus station, and besides, she did not have any money for tickets.

She had expected the announcement to give him relief, but he did not seem relieved.

"Pate said the trip was both ways." He was scowling.

"I know, but Pate didn't tell you about the children. I think us returning by bus will work out better."

He said, "Suit yourself," and pushed the cigarette lighter in with a hard thump.

It was nice to see that he was not happy about it.

Seconds of silence, louder even than it had been before, ticked past. Lacey began to feel like a foolish child. Now she was so embarrassed, she really would have to get them back home on the bus. She had dug her own hole.

The road rolled along beneath the massive Kenworth wheels, and they pushed on across the miles of open Texas panhandle. Anna had just required her second rest stop in less than two hours, and Lacey was handing each of the children a juice drink she'd purchased from a machine when Cooper grabbed one of the cans right out of her hand, set it on the floor and got the other, too.

"If we continue to make every rest stop between here and North Carolina, we won't get there till Easter," he said, definitely in a harsh tone.

"When are we goin' to get some lunch?" Jon asked. "I'm hungry."

"We don't get lunch," Cooper said. "We'll eat dinner tonight when we stop."

Lacey retrieved the cans from the floor. "If you're not plannin' to stop for lunch, these children need something to drink."

She fixed her eyes on him and silently dared him to argue. He didn't.

Reminded ten minutes later by Jon about a growing boy's hunger, Lacey produced homemade cookies from her tote bag. As she passed the sweets back to the children, she considered offering some to Cooper. But *he* was the one who'd refused to stop for lunch, she thought smartly. Let him smell the cookies and drool. Minutes later, she was shamed by her own five-year-old daughter.

"Mr. Cooper, would you like a cookie?" Anna asked in a hesitant voice, her hand extending a cookie as far toward Cooper as she dared.

Cooper's eyes came round, glancing at Lacey and then quickly at Anna. "Thank you," he said and took the cookie. His eyes went to the mirror, looking back at Anna. He almost smiled; Lacey was sure of it.

When he'd finished the cookie, Lacey offered him a slice of the pecan pie. "It's one of Gerald's."

"You got that in that bag?" he asked with surprise.

"Uh-huh. I cut it and wrapped each slice." She was digging it out of the bag. She unwrapped a piece, set it on a paper towel and handed it across to him. He took it, a distinctly sheepish expression on his face.

He liked sweets, Lacey thought. Highly pleased with the knowledge, she turned her face out the window. She had something to work with now. Call it a bribe, but she thought it more a way to build a bridge.

Traveling Companions

As Cooper had heard predicted, gray clouds closed in as the afternoon wore on. Reports came in from fellow truckers that north of them a storm was wreaking havoc, covering everything with a thick layer of ice and dumping snow in the mountains. It appeared the storm would stay to the north. Cooper hoped so.

Though she sat up front in the cab, Lacey said little, and she didn't have that friendly air she normally had. He guessed he couldn't blame her. He hadn't been exactly polite.

But he didn't think she'd had reason to say that she and the kids would return to Albuquerque by bus. If she thought that he was going to feel like the bad guy, she was mistaken. He was relieved. He was. But he was annoyed, too. He had put himself out for her, and he didn't see that she had to go changing the plan.

All of a sudden he came out with, "Watchin' TV?"

"What?"

"The kids…they're watchin' TV?" He felt around for his pack of cigarettes and kept his gaze steadily on the road.

"Yes. I think they'll nap," she replied. That was it, and she kept her gaze out the passenger window.

Fine. He liked quiet. He glanced down at his cigarettes and then over at her. He put the pack back into his pocket and reached for a bottle of water instead.

The next instant, he said. "You goin' to see your folks in North Carolina for Christmas?" Damn. It was like there was some sort of short circuit to his mouth.

"Yes." She nodded and hardly seemed to be looking at him.

Okay. He was not going to keep making an effort at conversation. He wasn't any good at it anyway.

Then she said, "The children have never met my parents. It's sort of a homecoming. I haven't been home since before Jon was born."

He glanced over to see a shy expression on her face. Her eyes met his for an instant, before they each looked away. Her eyes had been very green, like rye grass in spring.

"Ah…"

Now inability to speak struck him. And he had the oddest sensation of being aware of her breasts gently moving as she breathed.

"Cooper?"

"Yeah?" Hey, okay, here she was talking to him.

"Is Cooper your first name, your last, or what?"

He felt a smile coming up and out. "You been wonderin' about that, have you?"

"Yes, I have."

"Barry B. Cooper is the name."

He sent her a lazy glance. Her green eyes met his.

"Nice to meet you, Barry."

"Call me Cooper. I hate Barry."

Their eyes met again, and then each looked away out the windshield.

* * *

"You like George Strait?"

"Yes…I'd better, working at Gerald's."

He chuckled, his grin a flash of bright, even teeth beneath his dark mustache. He slipped a compact disc into the player. They had made an unspoken truce and fallen into actual conversation. With George Strait's voice in the background, they exchanged casual facts of their lives: Lacey had been divorced over four years— "Oh, yes, married only once"—and Cooper the same. "Once was enough." Lacey came from North Carolina and had ended up out in New Mexico because of her ex; Cooper actually and surprisingly had been born in eastern Tennessee, but had left there as a kid and lived all over the West.

They talked of Gerald's restaurant, and Cooper said he'd been stopping there somewhere around ten years; he had begun driving a truck twenty years before, at the age of eighteen. He'd known Pate almost that long.

"Pate came along, picked me up, dusted me off and set me on my feet."

There was a quality in his voice that drew Lacey's curiosity about the entire story, but he didn't elaborate, and she wasn't about to ask—at least she stopped herself before doing so. Her mind, however, was putting pieces together based on her own experiences and on all the stories she heard as a waitress in a busy truck stop. Listening to Cooper, she had a glimpse of a very lonely man, and she saw a reflection of her own well-deep loneliness. She guessed neither of them were rare cases.

The tires hummed along the highway, a second George Strait disc played, and they talked of baseball (a fondness they both shared), thick or thin pizzas and dog breeds (as children, each had possessed beloved dogs). Lacey looked at Cooper's profile. She watched his capable hands caress and maneuver the steering wheel—and imagined what those hands would feel like on her body.

In a flash of sudden awareness, she realized she had not thought of a man in such a way since well before Shawn had left.

Then she was looking into his dark eyes, and she had the embarrassing inkling that he knew exactly what she'd been thinking. That perhaps he had been thinking along the same lines himself.

George Strait sang out about eyes that can see.

Lacey turned to look out the side window.

They were one third of the way across Oklahoma when they stopped for dinner.

"I'm gonna check out the truck…you go on ahead," Cooper told her.

She herded the children, running and jumping in euphoria to be free, on into the restaurant. At the door, she looked back, wondering if he again would sit separately from them. She didn't suppose it mattered.

In the ladies' room, she combed her hair and put on fresh lipstick. Then she looked down to see Anna gazing up at her with large, dark, speculative eyes.

When they came out of the ladies' room, Cooper and Jon were waiting, side by side.

"It sure takes women a long time in the bathroom," Jon said.

To this Cooper drawled in a low voice, "Well, bud, they're a mite different, in case you didn't know that."

Jon rolled his eyes, and Lacey hid a smile.

They took a booth, Cooper and Jon sitting on one side, Anna and Lacey on the other. Cooper appeared only mildly ill-at-ease, bouncing his knees and holding on to his napkin, then dropping it and picking it up again. Jon's natural conversational ability took over, though, and soon the two were carrying on a conversation about cars and trucks and engines and racing, while Lacey and Anna were content to simply listen. Lacey was made aware of what her son missed by not having a man in his life. Very often Pate took them out to eat, yet, for whatever reason, Jon did not seem to relate to him in the avid manner that he related to Cooper.

Things seemed to be going great for the first time since they'd started out—until Anna spilled her cola down the back of a man in the adjoining booth.

They were preparing to leave, and Anna had been trying to move across the seat on her knees while carrying her glass. She bumped her elbow, sloshing the crushed ice and cold liquid, which came up in a perfect arc through the air and went neatly down the big man's collar.

The man let out a resounding holler. "What the hell?"

Lacey's waitressing instincts set her to grabbing napkins from the stubborn dispenser, which insisted on hanging on to them.

"Oh, I'm *so* sorry…so sorry." She began dabbing his neck and shirt, even as he moved out of the booth.

But then she looked into his face. *Oh, dear.*

She extended the wad of napkins and took a step backward.

Ignoring the napkins, the man rose from the booth, seeming to unfold into an enormous, redheaded giant, who was shaking the back of his shirt and sending little bits of ice clicking on the floor. Then he began bellowing words fit only for ships at sea.

Anna cowered behind Lacey's leg, sobbing. Lacey was about to fly at the man when a hand pressed her aside.

Cooper stepped in front of her. "That's enough." His command cut the air. "It was an *accident*. And you owe these ladies an apology."

The man, who had shut his mouth, peered at Cooper and then around him at Lacey and down at Anna. Then he glanced around the restaurant. Lacey looked, too.

Everyone was staring.

"Huh," the man said with disgust and began lowering himself back into his seat.

"I believe you forgot somethin'," Cooper said.

The big man's eyebrows shot up. Lacey, still behind Cooper's shoulder, tugged on his coat. But Cooper stayed planted.

"Pardon me...la-*dies*," the big man said in a low voice and with a bare glance, as he lifted a coffee mug to his lips.

Lacey turned Jon and took Anna by the hand.

The next instant, Cooper was beside them and scooping up a wide-eyed, sniffing Anna to carry her grandly from the room.

"Stop in here," he said in the lobby outside the restrooms, where he lowered Anna gently to the floor. "*All* of you. I don't want to have to stop again ten minutes down the road."

The incident had brought up all sorts of uncomfortable memories. Cooper didn't like to have memories. He tried to leave them behind by walking quickly away from Lacey and the kids. He tried to focus on checking out the rig again, walking around it and kicking the tires, hard.

But still, the memories swirled around him.

"Boy, you're gonna learn not to be stupid." "I'll teach you to keep your mouth shut." "Kids are meant to be seen and not heard." The faces changed, but they all were big and threatening, and Cooper had been small for a child, like Anna. He had always seemed to be clumsy. Until he

turned fifteen and suddenly he had muscles. He had been on his own since then.

"Hey, buddy."

Cooper was bending over, checking the cables. He looked over his shoulder and knew he had made a clumsy error in not paying more attention. The red-headed giant bore down on him. He barely had time to straighten before the man swung, his fist plowing into Cooper's cheek.

It didn't last long, and Cooper got in a few licks of his own before the hulk sent one final blow to the solar plexus that knocked Cooper sprawling on the pavement. Satisfied, the man hitched up his pants and lumbered away, leaving Cooper watching after him and trying to get a breath.

He was picking himself up when he heard Lacey's voice and running footsteps. "Cooper? What..."

He held up a hand and tried to quickly straighten his shoulders, though the movement hurt considerably. Tentatively, he felt the already swelling skin beneath his eye. He licked blood from the corner of his mouth.

"Oh, goodness..." Lacey, hovering, pressed a tissue to his mouth. Her eyes were close enough for him to fully see her long eyelashes. Her womanly warmth drifted out and around him. He enjoyed her ministrations for a brief moment, then came to himself and pulled away.

"It was that big guy from the restaurant, wadn't it, Coop?" the boy said. "How'd you do?"

"Well, he doesn't look too good, either," Cooper managed to get out. He wasn't about to tell the kid, or Lacey, that about the best he'd done was give the hulk a split lip.

"Here…put this on your eye…come on now."

He took the tissue she handed him and dabbed at a sore place near his eye. He remembered the contact with the pavement. He said, "Let's get in the truck."

"Cooper, maybe we should go to a hospital."

"Aw, Mom, Cooper don't need no doctor."

"Just get in the truck," he said, his breath giving out on him. He jerked open the driver's side door and hoisted himself up, leaving her standing there. She was still there looking up at him. He closed the door.

Seconds later, she and the kids were crawling in the passenger side.

When the little one, Anna, passed through to the

sleeper, she touched his shoulder. Her brown eyes were large and wet. "I'm sor-ry, Cooper."

"It's okay, kid." He winked with his good eye. "Everybody has accidents. That fella had no call to talk to you like he did, you hear?"

A spark he liked seeing came into her eyes, and she nodded.

Then he turned quickly away to focus on the gauges, which he didn't really see. No one had cared about his welfare for a long time. It made him as confused as a bear walking down a city street to see the kind of looks these three were giving him.

Cooper wasn't about to say he hurt all over, but Lacey saw it in his careful movements and the fleeting wince. She remained quiet, which seemed the safest course. But she felt so horribly responsible. Because of her, Cooper was likely having the worst trip of his entire life.

Fifteen minutes later, when they were well down the road, she brought a slice of pecan pie from her tote and offered it to him. A grin flashed, followed by a wince.

"Oh, dear."

"I can manage." He wasn't giving up the pie. He took it as his reward.

* * *

They continued across Oklahoma, through several long sections of cold rain, and stopped for the night at a motel just off the interstate in Henryetta. The clerk naturally assumed they were all together, husband and wife and children. Confusion ensued when Lacey and Cooper, instantly and talking at once, with interjections by Jon, tried to explain.

"You want a separate room for the children?" the clerk asked, when he could get a word in. His gaze moved rapidly from Lacey to the children to Cooper, pausing curiously on Cooper's black-and-blue eye.

"For the three of them." Cooper wagged his finger.

The clerk shot Lacey a questioning look. "Yes, one for me and the children."

"You got it now?" Cooper said sharply enough that Anna jumped.

"Yes, sir."

The clerk looked down and wrote on a card. "Just sign in here, ma'am. And here's your key. Room 154." He slid a key across the counter and then held one out to Cooper. "Here's yours, sir. Room 155."

Lacey marched the children down the row of doors

to their room, which was the second from the end. The last one was Cooper's. Right next to theirs.

She unlocked the door for the children, then went to the truck to get their bags. Five minutes later she found herself standing in front of her room, Cooper beside her, in front of his room. For some reason she didn't understand in the least, it was a very awkward moment.

Cooper twisted his key in the lock; Lacey pushed open her door. They paused and looked at each other. The flesh surrounding Cooper's left eye was the color of roiling thunderclouds.

"I'm so sorry about what happened back at dinner," Lacey said. "Does it hurt terribly?"

"It hurts, but I'll live." His dark eyes searched hers, as if seeking answers to something that puzzled him.

Anna called, "Mama, do I have to take a bath?"

"Good night," Lacey said to Cooper.

"Good night."

They each entered their own rooms. The two doors clicked closed at the same instant.

Needing time alone, Lacey got Jon and Anna into bed before taking her shower. After having risen so early, the children fell asleep as soon as they had settled who got which pillow. The ensuing silence was more than golden—it was heaven to Lacey.

As she leisurely undressed, she could hear the muffled sound of the television on the other side of the wall in Cooper's room.

She wondered what he was watching.

Was he a late-night or early-morning person? Did he like showers or baths? She continued to wonder as she stood beneath the massaging heat of steaming water. Would he think she had a good body?

Just as she turned off the water, she heard a peculiar knocking. *Someone rapping on the wall,* she realized, as she stood in the tub, rivulets of water running down her skin. *Cooper? Knocking out a rhythm on the wall?*

Hesitating only one self-conscious second, before throwing caution to the wind and rapping back, she imitated his rhythm. Then she held her breath.

The knock came again.

Lacey clamped a hand over her mouth, stifling her laughter. Fine thing it would be to wake the children and have to explain herself to them.

But it was hilariously funny. Two grown people engaging in a childish stunt. She couldn't believe Cooper would do such a thing. Not solemn, gruff Cooper, who'd spent most of the day treating her as if she wasn't there.

Suddenly curious, she knocked again and waited expectantly.

But no more knocks came from his side. Only silence.

Lacey was suddenly exhausted, and very lonely. When she crawled into the double bed beside Anna, she brought the extra pillow and hugged it tight to her chest.

Morning came much too early. Immediately upon turning off the alarm, Lacey discovered that the rumbling she heard was the Kenworth engine—already running. How revolting. It was still pitch black, for heaven's sake.

Allowing the children a few minutes' extra sleep, she threw on her clothes and ran across the parking lot to the large gas station minimart to get sweet rolls and milk to tide them over until breakfast. At the last minute, she bought a sweet roll for Cooper, too.

Cooper knocked at their door while Jon was still dressing. "Come on, let's go." He definitely sounded testy.

Lacey didn't bother to awaken Anna enough for her to dress but gathered her up in her arms and carried her to the truck. Without speaking, Cooper helped get Anna into the sleeper, then slipped into the driver's seat, while Lacey and Jon threw their baggage into the back.

When Cooper shifted the truck into gear without as much as a "good morning," Lacey wondered if the knocking she had heard the night before had happened at all. Had she imagined it?

When he switched off the radio in the middle of "Santa Claus Is Coming to Town," Lacey figured she had the answer to the question of whether he was a morning person or not.

And when he snapped at her to please stop that noise, calling attention to the fact that she was now unconsciously humming "Santa Claus Is Coming to Town," she called herself a saint for buying a dyed-in-the-wool Scrooge a sweet roll.

She gave him the roll, however, with every ounce of pleasantry she possessed. He scowled—but he took it. Heaven knew he needed all the sweetness he could ingest.

And it was true that every time she looked at his eye, which, although less swollen, remained the color of thunderheads, she told herself she could not forget what he had suffered on their account. What he was still suffering.

* * *

Cooper stopped a bit early for breakfast and varied his schedule to stop for lunch, too. He didn't know much about kids, but he knew enough about people to tell when two young ones were restless enough to explode. He was experiencing something similar himself. The feelings were unfamiliar and quite annoying. Never had he felt so keenly that he wanted to be anywhere but in the truck, stuck in one position behind the wheel.

He blamed it on not sleeping well. His face and various bruised parts of his body had throbbed too much. And he'd kept thinking about Lacey.

She was causing him no end of discomfort. Her green eyes were warm and full to bursting with life. Her scent drew him like a magnet. He couldn't seem to quit sneaking peeks at her body—at her sleek thighs hugged by blue denim, her breasts full and round beneath her soft sweater, her creamy neck and chin. Last night he had imagined in great detail what she looked like in the shower, just on the other side of his wall. He had not been able to stifle the very odd urge to knock on the wall. He had not done something so foolish in a very long time. Part of him had a sense of euphoria at his daring play, but the larger part was embarrassed. She must think him some kind of a nutcase. *He* thought himself some kind of nutcase.

Her knock in return had been immensely gratifying, and still was, but at the same time, it was threatening. He did not want her to get ideas about him. He did not intend to encourage any sort of relationship between them at all.

"I'm going to go ahead and see about fuel," he told Lacey, leaving the steak-burger he'd ordered only half-finished. "I'll meet you and the kids at the truck."

They were falling further and further behind schedule. Several rest stops this morning, now lunch. Good grief! They would be lucky to get to North Carolina before the new year.

He was stuffing bills into his wallet after paying for the fuel, when he looked through the station window into the small gift shop beyond. The kid, Jon, stood there examining something on a shelf—when he was supposed to have his butt out at the truck.

Cooper strode around the pumps and entered the store. "Come on, kid. This isn't a sightseein' tour, you know."

Something in the boy's expression stopped him. Stepping forward, Cooper saw the object of the boy's interest on the shelf: a woman's fancy brush-and-comb set. He looked at the boy.

"I was thinkin' of getting it for Mom," the boy said. "For Christmas."

"Well, get it and let's go."

The kid shuffled toward the door. "I'm goin'."

"Hey, you can take a minute to get that if you want."

The kid scuffed his feet. "Naw. I'm a bit short, and she probably wouldn't like it anyway."

"Here." Cooper pulled a wad of bills from his pocket and peeled off a twenty. "I'll advance you this, if you make certain my windshield's clean at every stop and be my general gopher, handling whatever I tell you."

The boy eyed the money, then cast Cooper a suspicious look. "Whatever you tell me?"

"Do you want the money or not?"

Jon hesitated another moment, then said, "You bet," and snatched the bill with one hand, reaching for the comb-and-brush set with the other. "I'll be out in a minute."

There was no pretense in the boy, Cooper thought, taking in how the boy had lit up like fireworks on the

Fourth of July. And an unusual glow spread within Cooper, as well.

"What is it?" Lacey asked when he reached the truck.

Only then did Cooper realize he was smiling. "Oh, nothin'." He looked at her for several long seconds, and she looked back. Then slowly that special smile of hers broke across her face, and Cooper recognized the one thing that made Lacey Bryant unique. She could smile and laugh over nothing at all.

Lacey knew something had transpired between Cooper and Jon. Jon returned to the truck with a secret grin for Cooper and a bag he immediately hid. Her Christmas present, she guessed. But where did Cooper fit into it? And why was he suddenly smiling, too?

Hearts Revealed

Lacey decided whatever had transpired between Jon and Cooper was definitely welcome. It had served to bring about a mellow atmosphere in the truck cab. Cooper no longer turned off the Christmas carols when they came on the radio, and he didn't even scowl when Jon and Anna began singing along with "Jingle Bells." Lacey dared to join in, and lo and behold, Cooper shot them all what could have passed for a grin—at least for him.

The next song was "Joy to the World," and they sang that, too, then listened attentively to the weather report. A winter storm was pushing down from the north. Although the weather forecasters did not think it would make it far into Arkansas and Tennessee, there was a chance.

"We'll get to Grandpa's and Grandma's by Christmas Eve, won't we?" asked Anna, who poked forward from the sleeper. "I have to be there to get the puppy Santa is bringin' me," she said, directing her words at Cooper.

"We'll get there for Christmas Eve, honey," Lacey said quickly.

"Santa's bringin' me a puppy," Anna told Cooper. When he didn't reply, she leaned toward him and peered at his face. "Cooper, didn't Santa bring you presents when you were a kid?"

Lacey sucked in a breath. He glanced quickly at Anna by way of his rearview mirror, then focused on the road.

"I guess he did…I can't remember."

"You said you didn't believe in him," Anna said.

Cooper looked at a loss—and quite annoyed. "I guess I don't."

"Maybe that's why you never got anything," Anna said.

Lacey unsnapped her seat belt. "Anna, honey, let's get in the back and take a nap. I'm really tired."

Lacey awoke and carefully extricated herself from the bed and the two sleeping children, and moved up front to the passenger seat. She might have imagined it, but she thought Cooper's expression a welcoming one. He instantly put out his cigarette, and the next moment he said, "I've got some coffee left, if you want some. There's a clean cup in there."

"Oh, thank you." She poured them each coffee, then pulled the last of the pecan pie from the tote bag and passed the piece to him.

"I don't want to take the last piece," he said.

"Go ahead. The kids have had plenty of sugar."

"Thanks." His expression was uncharacteristically and amusingly boyish.

Turning from this, she gazed out the window and watched the scenery roll past, taking note of the darkening skies. She felt tired all of a sudden, in the way one often did in the middle of some great expectation—the great expectation being for a special Christmas with her family, but now added to it was this trip with Cooper.

She had not expected any of this with him and had not had enough time to sort or even give name to her myriad of contradictory feelings.

She was sorting through a few of them, or trying to, at that moment, when Cooper said, "Guess your parents are anxious about you comin'."

"Oh…" She was a little startled by the fact that he had actually said something of a conversational nature. Startled, and a little thrilled. "My father doesn't know we're coming. It's a surprise—a ploy, really. My father and I haven't spoken in eleven years."

He cast her a glance, and, still carried by the delight that he had indicated a desire to converse, she went on to tell, in a low voice, the short story of being unwed and pregnant, and of her father's fury and her own resentment. "I'd always been the problem child. My getting pregnant was simply the last straw, so to speak."

His expression was curiously sharp. "The man's held his peace for eleven years. What if he doesn't bend now? Where will you stay?" That he appeared to grasp the implications of everything didn't surprise her. That he would care enough to ask the question was something of an amazement.

"We can stay with my sister and her family. We'll be okay," she added, as much for herself as for his seeming concern.

"And what about the kids? How do you think they'll feel if their own grandpa turns them away?" He fired the questions at her.

"I admit, I'm takin' a chance." The odd need to defend herself brought annoyance. "But I really think my father will not only bend but melt when he sees his grandchildren. Grandchildren have a way of doin' that to grandparents."

"Maybe for some," he said, in a somewhat sarcastic tone. In a brisk fashion, he shook a cigarette out of the pack and put it between his lips, then cut his eyes to her. His manner made her tense up and feel that she needed to find a positive response.

Before she could do so, he said, "My mother left me with my grandparents. They didn't want to be saddled with a six-year-old boy. I ended up bouncin' around in foster homes. Finally, at fifteen, I went back to see my grandpa. By then both my mother and grandma were dead, and my grandpa was alone. He was still just a mean old man who told me that he didn't have room for no bastard kid of a slut hangin' around."

"That's terrible," she managed to say, quite uncertain as to an appropriate response to such a sad tale.

"I survived."

She turned her gaze out the windshield. The skies and landscape seemed all shades of gray. Her thoughts went to her father and how he had looked the last time she had seen him. Hard and unrelenting. *Desperate* was a more accurate word.

"My father and I fought," she said. "A lot. But at least I know now that he loved me, in his way. He just didn't know how to show it."

Cooper's response was a grunt, which was proof that he had been listening, at least enough to know when she had finished her statement. However, a grunt fell somewhat short of satisfactory. She wanted him to respond. To talk with her. She had things to say. She did not want his sad and dismal attitude to hang over her.

"Not everyone in your life could have been like your mother and grandparents."

"I didn't say they were. But we were talkin' about grandparents. I knew a number of nice people as a kid, and still do—like Pate. There are a lot of good people in the world, but that doesn't make me blind to the fact that some people are just mean and don't ever change, like that guy back there yesterday with your girl. You forget that, you expect otherwise, and you're just askin' for a world of hurt."

Just then "Santa Claus Is Coming to Town" came out from the radio.

Cooper said, "You know, there's a lot of kids wonderin' why they have just about no gifts under their scrawny tree, and mom and dad in the kitchen drinkin' themselves into a stupor in celebration, while stores all over—owned and run by really good people—are all caught up in makin' their entire profit for the year."

She had wanted him to talk, she thought.

"You can focus on all of that," she said. "It's all true, but you can also look at the other side. People go so crazy with spending and decorating and giving gifts—with all the hype—because they need to do it. Christmas is the only time that such behavior is acceptable. Christmas at its heart is a time when everyone, even the most hardened criminal, can express the love that's in their hearts without feeling embarrassed or threatened."

"You ought to take off those rose-colored glasses," Cooper said with scorn. "What people call love is just lumps of fears and selfish motives in disguise."

"You are determined to see the dark side. You don't believe in Santa Claus, you don't believe in Christmas, and you don't believe in love. What do you believe in, Barry Cooper?" She was embarrassed to find her tone as sarcastic as his. How had they begun arguing? she thought with remorse.

"Myself," he said flatly. "And don't call me Barry."

The reply and tone pretty well squelched her remorse and caused her to prickle all over. She felt sorry for him, and angry because she felt sorry for him. She did not want to have pity for him. She wanted to admire him, and because she could not admire such a negative stance, she was angry.

Then came the clear thought: the devil of it was that underneath, just like Jolene and Pate had said, Cooper had a soft spot crying out to love and be loved.

And didn't everyone, even herself? She did not need him dragging on her own insecurities.

Cooper cast a glance at her. Her hands lay loosely in her lap in contrast to the vibrations he sensed, yet did not want to sense. He stubbed out his cigarette when it was only half smoked.

She was angry with him. Well, he didn't care. He'd just been being truthful. And he thought how she really did believe in all those pretty fantasies. He hoped she didn't get to Pine Grove and suffer a rude awakening. He hoped doubly so for the kids.

Suddenly he felt an overwhelming sense of protectiveness. He would punch the man, old or not, if the guy didn't do right by Lacey and those kids.

When he realized his thoughts, he almost stopped breathing. What business was it of his? *It wasn't any of his business at all.*

Traffic thickened the closer they came to Nashville, and it seemed a goodly number of fools were trying to kill themselves by pulling in front of the Kenworth.

Again Cooper had the sense of trouble with the brakes, and this sense was confirmed when they locked on him for several seconds. Ten miles farther down the road, he pulled off the interstate to a familiar truck-stop-and-motel complex on the outskirts of the city.

He was out and around to Lacey's side of the truck,

checking tires as he went, before she made it out of her seat. When her door swung open, it seemed the natural thing to raise his arms and help her down.

His hands slipped up beneath her short coat and closed around her waist. It was warm. She pressed her hands to his shoulders for balance, and Cooper lowered her slowly. A sweet fragrance floated from her hair. Then her thighs were brushing his, and he was looking into her eyes.

"Thank you," she said softly.

"Sure."

A movement from above caught his attention, reminding him that he remained with his hands at Lacey's waist. He let her go and looked up to find the boy, Jon, staring down at him with a curious and guarded expression. Cooper had the uncomfortable feeling the kid had read his mind.

"I'll follow you in a few minutes," he told Lacey. "I want to see if a mechanic here can take a look at the brakes."

"There's a problem?"

He glanced over to see her keeping silken strands of hair from blowing into her eyes.

"Just a small one. Nothin' to worry about." He felt her gaze on him as he walked quickly away.

Though the mechanic corrected the problem with the brakes in short order, Cooper elected to stay in the nearby motel. It was a neat, clean place, yet very inexpensive, which he knew would be a help to Lacey. Ordinarily, on a haul like this, Cooper would have spent the night in his truck.

"What about the storm?" she asked him over their coffee. "Several people here have said it isn't lookin' good."

Cooper said, "Driver over at the garage said up north some highways are being closed. But it hasn't turned south yet, and it may not. No sense worryin' about it beforehand. I'll keep a watch, and if the storm looks like it *has* turned this way, I'll get you and the kids, and we'll head on."

Her eyes were on his, and he didn't think she was thinking so much about the weather. He averted his gaze, not wanting her to read his mind.

More Surprises

With the heavy holiday traffic, they were lucky to get rooms—four doors apart.

Cooper's room was immaculate and modernly stark—bed, dresser, small portable television. He tossed his coat onto the bed, then turned on the set. Absently he watched a black-and-white rerun of *The Beverly Hillbillies* and smoked a cigarette. He put it out before he finished, the boy Jon's comments echoing in his mind. He really needed to give the things up.

He took the pack from his shirt pocket, saw it had two

cigarettes left, then crushed it and tossed it into the trash.

When he looked up, it was at his image in the mirror on the wall. Something caught his attention. He leaned closer, examining his face.

His bruised eye looked quite a bit better. It didn't hurt so much, anyway. Lacey must have gotten used to it, because around lunchtime she had quit getting that expression of guilt every time she looked at him.

Then he stared at his full face as if at a stranger. It was a man scowling. The cheeks were long and drawn. Tired, he thought. Tense from driving in the rig with passengers, kids and knowing their lives were his responsibility.

He rubbed his cheek, and then he knew what he saw in his image—his grandfather.

He didn't want to believe it, but now that he had noticed, the resemblance seemed to shout at him.

This idea so unnerved him that he turned quickly, snatched his coat off the bed and headed out the door, letting it slam behind him.

He strode along the edge of the road, hands deep in his pockets and collar turned up against the wind, heading toward the shopping center that was just across the highway overpass. Even with the cold, damp wind and cars whizzing past, slinging water on his pants leg, it felt good to be out in the open. The cold and wind helped to clear his mind of the memories that had been swirling around him ever since he had talked with Lacey about his past.

There was a Salvation Army bell ringer at the door of the discount store on the end of the mall, where he entered. Without breaking stride, he dropped a couple of dollars in the pot and continued on inside, maneuvering around people and searching and finding the aisle with the cigarettes. But when he reached them, he heard again in memory the boy's blasted refrain: *You shouldn't be smokin'*.

Hands stuffed firmly in his coat pockets, he walked away, calling himself all kinds of a dope and debating about going back.

And then he found himself distracted by an array of stuffed animals. Not much of an array, as the shelf was empty in spots. But there was this one wrinkled puppy with a vest and bow tie sitting all by itself, almost as if waiting. He thought the little girl Anna would like it. And it didn't cost all that much, he told himself as he went to the checkout counter.

He was a prosperous man now, very far from the fifteen-year-old boy who had stood in the yard, with all of his things in a frayed duffel bag, facing his grandfather and wanting somewhere to belong. His grandfather's attitude had been that Cooper would come to no good, but he had determined to prove the old man wrong. He had made a place for himself in the world. He owned his second brand-new top-of-the-line Kenworth and lived in a spacious, upscale apartment when he wasn't traveling the road. He could pretty much buy anything he wanted, had a good name in the business, savings in the bank. He was a respected man with a secure future. Yes, he had proved the old man wrong.

For the first time it occurred to him to wonder where his grandfather's hate-filled attitude about him had come from. He had never done one single thing to the old man.

The thought came softly and gently, like a crack in dark clouds, where sunbeams broke through. While standing there in the middle of the busy shopping mall, surrounded by the rich sights of Christmas in every shop window and familiar carols ringing from speakers all around, Cooper felt the first stirring of compassion that he had ever experienced for his grandfather. He thought of how much his features resembled those of the old man, and saw his grandfather as once a kid and then a young man, too.

In one swift moment, he knew that his grandfather had been a pitiful man eaten up with whatever had hurt him, and that none of it had had anything to do with Cooper, not then and not now.

A bunch of boys came running past. One brushed into Cooper and said, "Uh, sorry, sir," and was gone.

Cooper was a sir, not the once-needy boy anymore. And life had been good to him, far better than he had heretofore realized.

He looked down at the sack containing the stuffed dog. Of course, he couldn't buy that and not get something for the boy. Breaking into swift strides, he headed for the toy store across the mall, where he perused the shelves with a growing eagerness that felt a little strange.

The shelves were bleak, with most of the toys sold out. Determined to get something special, though, he meandered back through the mall and a number of stores, until finally coming to the boy's clothing section in a department store.

There he spied a black jacket with the Dale Earnhardt Junior racing insignia on it. Size?

"Hey, kid," he said, sizing up a boy standing several feet away. "How old are you?"

"'leven."

"Well, you're about the right size. Here's five bucks. Try this jacket on for me, okay?"

"You bet!" A smallish hand snatched the bill, and the boy proceeded to instruct Cooper in the facts of fashion for boys. "It's gotta be baggy, man. You want this one."

As Cooper left the checkout counter with another shopping bag, he experienced rising spirits and the daring thought to find something for Lacey, although he couldn't imagine what and felt foolish for even considering it.

He paused in front of a lingerie store, gazing at a lace-and-silk gown on a mannequin. The next instant a saleswoman was leaning into the window, draping a tiny sexy nightie into the display. She raised an eyebrow at him.

Feeling his face turn fiery, Cooper shook his head and moved along.

Maybe perfume? Not a chance.

Maybe a candle? Nah.

Best not to get her anything. It was understandable that he would buy for the kids at Christmas, but he didn't want Lacey to get the wrong idea about him buying her something.

Then, passing a gift shop, he looked in the window and spied a crystal-ball snow scene. The ball was a bit larger than his gearshift knob, sat atop stained oak, and had a miniature ceramic Christmas tree inside, with colorful presents underneath it and an angel on top.

After hesitating only a moment, he went in to buy it.

When he got back to his motel room, he set his packages on the bed and gazed at them. He wondered at what was happening to him.

He could no longer deny that something *was* happening to him.

He looked again in the mirror, jutting his face forward and searching his image. This time he found no trace of his grandfather.

Likely he was just imagining all of it. He really had gotten to thinking too much since he had dragged up all that stuff about his past. That was why he never liked to think or speak about it.

He patted his shirt pocket and came up empty. Dang,

he wished to have bought the cigarettes. He did not think now a good time to quit, despite the boy harping at him.

He walked down to the motel's office, passing Lacey's room as he went. Light showed around the edges of the heavy drapes. Sounded like a television going.

In the lobby, he got a cigarette package out of the machine. The clerk had a small television going, and he paused for a look at a weather report.

"Boy, they're gettin' it up north a-ways," the clerk said. "Closed the St. Louis airport."

"Really? Is it still stayin' north?"

"So far. We're gonna get some sleet, maybe heavy ice in places."

On his way back to his room, he got a Coke from the machine. He kept looking at Lacey's window, with the light around the edges. He did not intend to stop.

But he did, as if his feet had a mind of their own, and the next instant, he raised his hand and knocked softly.

Lacey, sitting in the chair right next to the door on the other side and staring mindlessly at the television, about jumped out of her skin at the sound. She immediately thought of Cooper and some possible emergency.

Eyes anxiously going to the children asleep in the two double beds, she attempted to answer the door before another knock that could wake one or both of them. But the blanket she had wrapped around her legs got all tangled, with the result that she pitched forward and almost fell on Anna, managing at the last moment to twist and end up plunking on the floor instead.

Outside, Cooper heard the thudding noise just as he was about to knock a second time. His hand froze in midair.

Lacey made it to standing again and frantically scrambled to the window to pull back the curtain. Cooper's face was only inches away, and his eyes seemed to widen in surprise at seeing her.

She dropped the curtain, smoothed her hair and clothes, and calmed herself before removing the security chain, as quietly as possible, and opening the door.

"Hi," she said, studying him intensely for signs of trouble. "Is there a problem? Has the weather worsened?"

"Uh…not yet. But it could. I just thought I should tell you. It's gonna sleet, and it may get up a good ice storm in some places they're sayin' now."

He gazed down at her, and she knew he had not

stopped to talk about weather. She stepped out, he moved enough to let her, and she pulled the door closed behind her.

"Kids asleep?" he asked.

She nodded. "They were exhausted. They may sleep in the truck, but this is all a lot for them." Folding her arms, she hugged herself against the bitter wind.

Cooper moved over to shield her with his body, an act that struck her deeply. She began to shiver, and not all from the cold.

Though she couldn't clearly see his eyes or assess his expression because of the dim light on the porch, she felt the warmth of him. She told herself it was because he blocked the wind. She told herself he couldn't be attracted to her, at the same time that she knew very well he was. And that she wanted him to be, wanted him in a way that she had not wanted a man in many years.

"Look, Lacey," he said, "you'd arranged to ride back to Albuquerque with Pate. I'll be goin' back, just like he would. You and the kids might as well come along."

Her mind was still back at hearing him say her name, at the way he drawled out the word. Finally she said, "Think you could stand the kids?"

"Hey, it's only for a few days." He almost grinned.

His eyes were very dark as he gazed at her, and his grin faded completely. The wind snatched at his thick hair, and the yellow glow of the porch light magnified the bruise around his eye. Lacey caught the scents of cigarette smoke, leather and faint cologne. His gaze moved from her eyes to her lips, then back up to her eyes again.

"Here, take my coat," he said in a husky voice. "Don't want you to catch pneumonia."

She shook her head and protested, "Then you'll be cold," but he was already shrugging out of it.

He slipped it around her with awkward motions, one hand still holding the Coke. The back of his hand caressed her neck, and she knew without doubt that he'd done it on purpose. Her breath caught in her throat. His eyes were on her intently.

He said, "The first time I saw you in Gerald's I wanted to kiss you."

He seemed as amazed by his words as she was. His eyes were all over her face, and her heart was beating like running horses.

She said, "The first time I saw you, I wanted to touch your cheek to see if you were as cold as you looked."

He shook his head and chuckled, looked away and back at her.

"I didn't want you to come on this trip."

"I could tell…just barely, but I could tell."

His teeth showed for an instant. Then, intensely, "Pate never said…is there anything between you and him?"

She shook her head. "Not like you're thinkin'. He's a good friend."

He seemed to relax, to take a breath. "I haven't meant to be an ass. I'm just not good with kids."

"It's okay. I know we came as a big shock to you. You are, though—good with kids." He looked skeptical, and she said, "You really are."

Again they gazed at each other. He got this rather ironic and fearful and hopeful grin. She raised her hand to touch his cheek. She felt the stubble of a beard on his warm skin.

"You're warm," she whispered.

His head came down, slowly, slowly, and his arms slipped around her, slowly, slowly, and she wrapped her arms around his neck, not too very slowly but with a great sigh.

Then he was kissing her. Hard and demanding, lips pressing and hearts pounding.

When they at last broke apart, she said breathlessly, "It's been a long time since I've been kissed."

He gazed down at her with something of a puzzled expression. His chest was heaving, too. He touched her lips with his thumb, and then bent his head and kissed her eyes softly. Then her lips, softly. A kiss of goodbye.

He stepped away from her, reached behind her and opened the door to her room. "Good night," he said, giving her that almost-grin.

"Good night," Lacey managed to say as she handed him his coat.

She slipped through the door, closed it, and leaned against it, her heart beating hard beneath her ribs.

Later, when she lay in bed, she pulled the pillow against her chest and struggled with the emotions of a woman overwhelmed about a man.

She was awakened by a loud pounding on the door. "Lacey…Lacey!"

While she struggled to find her way from beneath the covers, she heard the door open and Jon's voice. Freed at last from the blankets, she stumbled to her feet to see Cooper standing there.

"What time is it?" She had trouble focusing, but she could see behind Cooper's head that it was still black outside. She was tired of getting up before the chickens.

"Four-fifteen," Cooper said. "The storm is on its way, and we gotta hustle if we want to get to Pine Grove by evenin'." Turning, he strode away.

Within twenty minutes Lacey had herself and Jon dressed, their bags gathered and Cooper was helping a sleepy Anna into the truck.

"Is that snow?" Lacey paused and looked upward into the light of the pole lamp.

"Yes," Cooper said. "Let's go."

Cooper had thoughtfully bought coffee, milk and sweet rolls for the early hours, and at nine they stopped to refuel and took just long enough for a quick breakfast. It began to snow in earnest, big heavy flakes. The report was icy rain to the east, which would be more dangerous than snow.

Lacey's gaze kept straying to Cooper's profile, then down to his hands on the wheel, her mind having the perverse tendency to dwell on the feel of his lips on hers. He didn't seem to remember. His focus was on the storm.

He likely kissed women on a frequent basis, she thought.

Cooper isn't the marrying kind, Jolene had said. And Lacey didn't think he was *her* kind, either.

Her insides became tighter and tighter as she sat and watched the outside world grow whiter. When she cautioned the children to be quiet, she had to grit her teeth to keep from yelling. The worries swirled in her mind. Would they make Pine Grove by evening? Somehow she wasn't in as much of a hurry now. She dreaded saying goodbye to Cooper. Would her father accept them upon arrival? Would she be able to borrow enough from Beth to get them home again? No way could she ride with Cooper. He would know how she felt about him, and she would feel a fool. Would Cooper ever be just another customer to her again?

The traffic thickened in the mountains, as did the falling snow, piling up inch by inch over the ice that had come before it. Repeatedly Cooper swore under his breath at vehicles pulling in front of him, slamming on their brakes, slowing dangerously. He commanded the children to get into the bed of the sleeper and stay there, and he checked twice to make certain Lacey had her seat belt buckled.

Just past noon they were forced to leave the highway.

It had been closed ahead because of ice and drifting snow. The good news was it was expected to be cleared within the hour.

"Good a time as any for lunch," Cooper said, bringing the big truck to a stop in a restaurant parking lot.

He stretched his arms, and Lacey saw the lines of strain around his eyes. For a brief moment she dared to meet his gaze. With surprise, she saw an unusual softness in his dark eyes as they met hers. The same softness she'd seen there when he had kissed her, and an intimate smile, all for her.

"Are we gonna make it to Grandpa's by Christmas Eve, Cooper?" Anna asked in a worried voice as they trudged through the wet snow to the crowded restaurant.

"It *is* Christmas Eve," Jon told her.

She looked up at Cooper, who paused and looked down at her. "I'll get you there tonight, squirt, if I can at all."

Then, in a fluid, surprising motion, he swooped Anna up into his arms. "Let's keep your feet dry. Don't want to make your cold worse on vacation."

White Christmas

Cooper went off to check highway conditions. He returned and slipped into the booth. "They've cleared one lane going east. And it's slick out there," he told Lacey. "I think we can handle it, but there is some danger." He gazed at her with a raised eyebrow.

His consulting her came as a bit of a surprise. She gazed at him, and then looked at her children.

Anna said with all practicality, "We have to get to Grandpa's, Mama, or else Santa won't know where we are."

"Cooper can handle it, Mom," Jon said with confidence.

"Of course he can…and of course we're goin' on." The looks Cooper and Jon exchanged did not escape her notice. Boys and men, she thought.

Then Cooper lifted Anna and carried her out to the truck. Jon slid on his shoes across the lot. Lacey prayed, *I trust in You, Lord.*

The big truck rolled down the entrance ramp and into the single lane of traffic, all going at an amazingly good clip, to Lacey's mind. From the sleeper, Anna and Jon poked their heads out and sang, "Jingle Bells…"

Cooper actually grinned.

Lacey peered hard through the windshield. The hard north wind made a muffled roaring sound, and the windshield wipers thumped rapidly as the Kenworth sliced through the swirling white gloom. The CB radio crackled occasionally with reports of the highway conditions from drivers heading both east and west. Music from the radio provided a low background to it all. Twice, on two different stations, they heard "White Christmas," and Jon and Anna sang along.

It bothered Lacey this time. She told the children to please get back in the sleeper and stay there.

"Where's your Christmas spirit?" Cooper said, giving her a wink.

The snow began to blow back on the road faster than the plows could keep it clear. Repeatedly, the truck plunged through drifts that completely obliterated the pavement. Lacey caught occasional glimpses of two other rigs up ahead. Directly in front of them was a red station wagon, a blessing to follow with visibility so poor.

Though she could feel the tug of the wind and the occasional sliding of the truck, Lacey strangely did not feel terribly anxious. She felt a certainty they were going to be all right, and this caused her to worry if she was being neglectful of worrying.

She glanced over at Cooper. All his attention was focused on his driving, and it was as if he were attached to the truck, anticipating its every movement. She suspected, by the rapt look on his face, that he secretly loved the challenge of driving in such abominable weather.

It had begun to grow quite dim when it happened. Lacey had actually been drowsing when a car came pushing around them in a rare wide spot in the road. As Cooper braked slightly and struggled to keep the Kenworth on the road, he cursed under his breath, which brought Lacey up in her seat to see the car's taillights disappear immediately into the gloom. She strained to see, expecting to find the sedan nose first in a snowbank on the shoulder, as they'd seen many others.

She glanced at Cooper and saw a worried frown crease his brow. He let out a curse, and Lacey looked again out the windshield to see red taillights getting rapidly larger.

Cooper, who had instinctively slowed his already crawling rate of speed, reacted immediately and carefully. Coming down on the brakes too fast could jackknife the trailer and even overturn the entire rig. The red lights seemed to grow larger right in front of his eyes.

The damned car was *stopped* in the middle of the road!

He applied the brakes as hard as he dared. The trailer began to skid back and forth across the narrow strip of road, dragging the truck with it. Then, in frustrating slow motion, despite Cooper frantically turning the wheel, the truck left the highway and plowed its way down the sloping ground, sending snow up and out in a giant wave.

The truck came to a gentle rest, snugged all around in the snow.

"Lacey...Lacey, you all right?" He ran his gaze over her, and relief surged through him when she appeared only mildly shaken.

She nodded and jerked around. "Anna? Jon?"

The children came scrambling forward, not scared but excited as all get-out, the way kids could be. Cooper let out a breath and ran a hand through his hair. "I'll have a look."

"I wanna go," Jon said, eagerly throwing Cooper's coat at him and scrambling not to be left behind.

Cooper knew beforehand, though, that there would be no getting the truck up on the road again without help.

They got back into the cab along with cold wind and swirling snowflakes.

"What about that car in the road? Are they all right?" Lacey asked.

Jon answered. "The stupid car's gone, Mom."

Looking thoroughly disgusted, Cooper got on the CB and began calling for help. Quite quickly the answer came: Help would be sent as soon as they could get through. For now, wait.

"I'm hungry," Jon said.

"I'm cold," Anna said.

"Guess I agree with both," Cooper said, a dry grin twisting his lips.

Lacey laughed, and laughed again. Suddenly she was absurdly happy. "I think I can fix both things," she said.

They were all safe, just as she'd known they would be. Thanks to her motherly inclinations, they had plenty of refreshments. The truck's engine continued to purr, putting out heat, and they had plenty of clothes and blankets. They were snug as could be.

From the big tote bag, Lacey pulled cookies and sweet rolls that she had Jon pop into the microwave oven. As she passed out napkins, her hand brushed Cooper's. Their eyes met.

For the first time in years, Lacey thought, she was sharing the company of her children with a handsome man she had come to care a lot about.

For the first time in years, Cooper thought, he was not spending Christmas Eve alone and lonely.

After they'd all eaten, Lacey tucked herself and the children into the warmth of the bed. When Anna began worrying about Santa Claus, Lacey tried to divert her by telling stories about both children when they had been babies. She succeeded in getting Cooper to smile, while he appeared not to listen.

Soon Anna and then Jon fell asleep. Lacey laid her head back, lulled by the gentle rumbling of the diesel engine. Idly she gazed at Cooper, smoking a cigarette up in the driver's seat. She let her eyes roam over him, wondering how they had come to this point together.

When she noticed him rubbing his arms as if cold, she said, "Might as well join us. There's room." She wriggled herself and Anna over, indicating the empty space at the end of the bed.

Cooper looked at her, then sort of grinned. "Think I will. We've got a long night ahead."

Lacey leaned toward Anna, trying not to get too familiarly close to Cooper. It was impossible, of course.

Cooper slipped an arm around her shoulder. "It's okay. I promise I'm not a man to take advantage," he said, and then added sweetly, "At least not in front of witnesses."

After a moment's hesitation, Lacey decided she wasn't a person to *miss* an advantage. She settled into Cooper's offered shoulder.

It felt good, almost remarkably so.

She realized that she had never before experienced

such a feeling as she was at that moment, relying on Cooper totally.

She wondered what he felt, if anything. What was he thinking? His heart beat against her arm, and he was so wonderfully warm. She drifted off into the sweetness of the moment, a special Christmas gift.

Motion and hushed whispers woke her. Good heavens! She had fallen fully asleep. Cooper was gone from beside her, and Jon was shaking her leg with some urgency.

"Mama..." Jon said in an uncertain tone.

"Santa!" That was Anna in a strange voice.

"Well, I'll be dogged..." That was Cooper.

Lacey struggled to get to her feet and into the cab, peering around Cooper and Jon to see what everyone was staring at out the passenger-seat window.

Santa Claus.

Santa Claus?

Yes, it was. The faint glow from the cab spilled out upon his very jolly and white-whiskered face. Light snow fell on the velvet and fur cap on his head. He was grinning and peering back at them.

Anna rolled down the window. "Hi, Santa! Hi! Do you have my puppy?"

"Oh, missy, it's too cold out here for a puppy," Santa said.

Lacey thought maybe she was dreaming.

The Santa was saying, "Let's see…puppy…" He pulled a paper from his pocket and looked at it. "Yep, one puppy for…" He peered at Anna. "…for Annie."

"Anna," Anna corrected.

Now, how did he guess so close? Lacey would have bet a month's tips that his beard was real, as was his near shoulder-length white hair. His coat was black, but the pants beneath were deep, royal red.

"That's right. And you'll get him, but it'll be a little later. Live puppies are a tricky present. I always have to work that out. He's comin', but right this minute you need to get out of this cold, yes you do, missy. There's Mountain View Lodge just up the way about three 'r four miles. I can get you there, but I got to hurry. I got lots to do tonight, don't cha' know."

Several yards away sat Santa's odd-looking wagon-sleigh, pulled by two draft horses blowing steam in the cold air. Lacey heard bells. Peering harder, she realized there were bells on the horses' harness.

Anna wanted to know where Santa's reindeer were. "Where's Rudolph?"

"He's takin' a break. He's been workin' for eight solid hours, darlin," Santa told her heartily. "And in this area, ol' Jim and Tom know the way. I borrowed them from a friend, while my reindeer eat a bite."

By then Cooper had his coat and hat on and was getting out of the truck. Anna started after him, and Lacey had to pull her back and get her bundled up and gather their bags. Anna would hardly be still and kept straining to see Santa, who had gone over to his sleigh with Cooper.

Cooper and Santa returned together. Santa took a very excited Anna to his sleigh, and Jon followed along, cueing Santa by saying, "I told her all about your magic sleigh that can go faster than anything on earth, and how the world turnin' like it does works in your favor."

Cooper helped Lacey get her bags down, then began to shut down and lock up the truck. Lacey was struggling toward the sleigh, when Santa returned to help her.

"Who are you?" she asked the pink-cheeked man in a whisper.

"Don't you know, missy?" he answered. Then, "Oh, I see you don't believe I'm Santa."

"Well, yes…yes, I do…but…who are you?"

There actually was a storybook twinkle in his eye so bright that she could see it in the dimness. In fact, there *was* a magical quality about him. Although, she found anyone coming to their rescue right then quite magical.

He said, "Darlin', maybe you could accept the explanation of an old cabinetmaker who enjoys makin' sure that the tykes up in these back hollers—them that sometimes don't have much—don't get forgotten at Christmastime. And it 'pears that this year I've had a bit of search and rescue thrown in, too. I've already hauled five people out of various predicaments. Gettin' behind schedule…I hope he knows…." His voice trailed off.

"Busy night for Santa," Lacey said.

"Yep…but not a one hurt, thank God. And the most fun I've had in twenty years." The man chuckled in a very merry fashion.

"Would you…" Lacey lifted the travel bag containing her presents. "Could you give the children and Cooper their gifts for me?"

"You betcha'. You just leave it all to me. That's my job, after all, you know." His cheeks *were* rosy in the dim light still shining from the cab.

The curious wagon-sleigh had lanterns on each of the four corners. Anna was tucked beneath a thick blanket in the front seat next to Santa, while Lacey and Cooper, with Jon between them, managed to sandwich themselves into the second seat, with all of their bags around their feet.

Looking behind the seat, Lacey saw the area filled with something that was covered with a blanket and tied in with cord.

"Gee-haw," Santa called to the horses, and the sleigh was off through the night, with bells jingling on the harness and snowflakes falling softly upon them. Anna chatted happily with Santa about what she and her friends wanted, and he told her about children he had already visited. Cooper's arm came around behind Jon, and his hand took hold of Lacey's arm that was holding on to Jon, who repeated again and again, "Man, this is cool. Just too cool."

Lacey silently agreed. It was a magical experience she would share with her children long after they grew up and she grew old. She was so glad that she had made the trip, just to have this experience.

Nevertheless, when the lights of the lodge finally

shone through the snowfall, she was glad to see them. She was frozen clear through. When they came to a stop beneath the wide portico, she found she had to lean heavily on both Santa and Cooper to get out of the wagon and stand straight.

"Now, let's see what we have here," Santa said, producing a red corduroy bag from beneath the wagon's front seat and crouching to Anna's size in a manner that seemed that of a much younger man, Lacey thought.

Cooper felt a rush of pleasure when Anna squealed over the stuffed dog he'd bought her, and Jon insisted on trying on his jacket right then and there. But mostly it was the wonderment in Lacey's eyes as she held the crystal ball snow scene that moved him. The eyes she turned to him had tears in them and were filled with so much pure happiness that he had to look away.

When Santa began handing out wrapped packages, Cooper realized that there were more presents than the ones he'd given the old man. With amused amazement, he realized Lacey had done the same as he. His amazement tripled when Santa placed a small package into his hands.

Lacey had bought him a present!

He stared at the bright red package with the gold ribbon. He hadn't had a real present for years. There had been precious few of them throughout his entire life. He looked up to find Lacey gazing at him, a trembling smile on her lips. Feeling a whole lot the way he had when he'd lost control of the Kenworth, he smiled back and stuffed the package into his coat pocket. He would wait until he was alone to open it.

It turned out that Santa had his own presents for Anna and Jon. Her arms full, Anna looked at Santa. "What about my puppy?"

"Like I told you, that there's a special present, little Miss Anna. You can't be haulin' a puppy all over on vacation. You'll be gettin' it a bit later, when you're on your way home."

Lacey wished he had not promised an exact time. She cleared her throat in a disapproving manner, which was all the satisfaction she could allow herself.

"O-kay," Anna said to Santa, with a trace of disappointment, but clear, trusting eyes.

Santa ruffled her hair, bade them all goodbye and climbed into his sleigh. With jingles and creaks and a thunderous *"Merry Christmas!"* he drove away.

Cooper stood beside Lacey and watched the wagon-sleigh be swallowed up by the night. He felt a tug on his coat. It was Anna.

"I told you there was a Santa Claus," she said solemnly.

"Yes, you did."

"Do you believe now?"

"Yes, I believe."

"That's why you got a present," she said pertly, and broke into a run for the lodge's lobby. "I want to open my packages!"

"Watch the steps, Anna!" Lacey called. Then she murmured playfully, "How do you suppose Santa knew where to find us?"

"Santa knows everything," Jon said with his usual know-it-all expression.

There wasn't any time to be alone and talk, not in the way she wanted to talk to him. Not that she really knew exactly what she would say to him. She needed to thank him for the snow globe, but she could not seem to get the words out. Every time she thought of the gift, she felt awash with emotion and was afraid she might even start crying. It was silly, really, and probably it was best that the children were there all through a meal in the restaurant and then going to their rooms, which they were really lucky to get in the storm. In fact, the clerk said they were the very last two rooms, far in the back and a bit mildewy smelling.

At his door, he said, "Good night," and across the hall at her door, she said, "Good night," and they went into the rooms and shut the doors, each giving a resounding *clack!*

She kept looking at the snow globe. Shawn had given her a few presents, things like kitchen knives, a blender, a decorative tissue holder. Good grief, life had just moved along, day after day, and she had ended up here, a woman entering her thirties with no worthwhile romantic memories or gifts, until now.

Thanking Cooper took upper place in her mind. She sat on the side of the bed and reached for the phone to call his room and express her gratitude, which was the polite thing, after all.

Then she dropped her hand.

She did this same action three more times, while the kids got their baths and played all around with their Christmas toys. They were higher than kites.

That Cooper did not call *her* began to annoy her. The least he could do was call, after she had given him a gift, too.

All of a sudden the phone rang and about scared her to death. She snatched up the receiver as if it were an emergency. It was Cooper, of course. If she had been alone, she might have danced.

After they exchanged hellos, there was a long pause, and then he said, "Are the kids asleep yet?"

"Oh, no…they're too excited, what with a crash, a ride with Santa, and gettin' their gifts. They might be awake all night."

"Oh," came the response and a sigh of the disappointed sort, which was gratifying. "I asked a couple of people down at the desk if they could tell me the name of our Santa. Thought I might send him some money, you know, for all the help. But it seems no one has heard of him."

"Really?"

"Seems that no one knows of any Santa who goes around givin' gifts to kids around here. I wish I'd gotten his name."

She got up and moved to the window, putting distance between her and the children. They were so into their cutting up, though, they were not likely to hear. "I don't think he wanted us to have his name. I asked, but he just put me off."

"I kind of like it like this, anyway," she admitted, daring to add, "I'm awfully glad we came on the trip with you. I wouldn't have wanted to miss this…but I hope your truck is okay. I wouldn't want…"

"Oh, the rig's fine. Just stuck. I've already been makin' some calls. The storm is lettin' up, and we'll get back on the road quick as we can tomorrow. I'll get you and your kids to your family, Lacey."

"I know you will." She had this moment where she realized she had forgotten the entire reason for the trip.

Then Anna flung herself and her big stuffed dog onto Lacey's bed, saying, "Ma-ma…maaa-ma."

"Just a minute, honey. Oh, not you, Cooper—I was talkin' to Anna."

Jon threw himself down beside his sister, and both children regarded Lacey with the expectancy of children requiring attention.

"I guess I better go. They're gettin' tired."

Cooper said he would see her in the morning, and the line clicked dead before she hung up on her end.

* * *

The room was faintly lit by the dim bulb in the bathroom, whose weak glow fell through the thin opening of the door and cut across the room. Anna slept deeply, with a little wuffling snore. In the other bed, Jon was a tangled knot somewhere beneath the blankets.

Lacey, curled on her side beside Anna, gazed at the snow globe. It sat on the nightstand, in front of the clock, which read one-sixteen. The glowing red digital numerals seemed to light the globe, like a prism.

Reaching out, Lacey gently shook the globe, then lay there watching the sparkles drift and float magically downward. The angel atop the tree shimmered as if alive.

Across the hall, Cooper sat on the edge of his bed, working to change out the buckle on his belt for the one Lacey had given him. His belt was custom-made from a leather maker in Santa Fe, the tooled leather far more valuable than any of the buckles he ever used with it, which could be changed by a snap. Only the snap was proving resistant. Cooper had to pry it open with his knife.

He got the old buckle off and put the one Lacey had given him in its place. He gazed at it. Antiqued brass, it was inexpensive, but his style. She had bought him something that was his style, he thought, holding it out to look at it.

Memories marched across his mind of the hundred or so times over the past few years that he had gone into Gerald's and Lacey had greeted him and served him his meal. She always smiled at him and asked how he was. He most generally answered, "Fair to middlin'. And you?" She would say, "Better than I ought to be," in that chipper way and with that smile that lit up the room. She brought him everything just the way he liked it, waiting until his coffee cup was nearly empty before filling it again, telling him how the chili or the steak was that day. He had seen her cut her hair short and grow it out. He had seen her a hundred times plug coins in the jukebox, playing snappy tunes by Alabama and dancing across the room, and when she seemed melancholy, an old ballad by Don Williams to which she would hum. He had seen her habit of tucking her hair behind her ear, and the graceful way she walked and the extra care she gave people.

It struck him that while he had not known particulars such as about a husband or children, he did know the woman. He didn't know what to make of that thought.

He blinked, and the memories vanished. He found himself staring at the belt buckle. Almost like it was a snake that might bite him, he tossed the belt aside on the bed and got up to find a cigarette. He had wanted one since supper but had determined to give them up. He figured six hours was long enough for a respectable start on no-smoking.

He had no sooner lit up than his gaze fell to a small sign on the wall: Non-smoking room. Alarm will sound.

Instinctively he looked upward and saw the smoke alarm, as well as the sprinklers. He sprinted to the window, threw it up and fanned the cold fresh air to help it inside, while he waited to see if an alarm would go off. After a few seconds, he relaxed and finished his cigarette by puffing the smoke out into the cold, black night.

When he finished, he shut the window, and went to take a shower and get ready for bed.

The next morning, up before dawn to start locating someone to get his rig back on the road, Cooper changed out the buckles on his belt again, returning to the old one. He reached into the trash can and got the box for the brass one Lacey had given him, put the buckle back into it, and tucked the box deep down into his duffel bag.

Ties that Bind

The next day the sun came out in a clear blue sky. The storm was gone as gone could be. Had it not been for the snow and ice—snow drifted in some places to five feet, it was reported and shown on television—it would have been as if the storm had never occurred. The day was even warming so much that the snow began to melt on the pavement and dribble off roofs.

Lacey kept reminding the kids that it was Christmas Day, but they had had enough of Christmas, having had all their excitement the previous evening. The day ahead definitely seemed anticlimactic, if not a total bore, what with having to travel more. Anna kept wondering dejectedly about her puppy, and Jon could not seem to be still.

For Lacey's part, she kept thinking about the snow globe gift from Cooper and having some expectations. The first of these had been a little squashed, when her only contact with Cooper that morning had been in two rather quick and terse telephone conversations, in which he informed her that he was off to have the truck hauled back onto the road, and then to tell her he had succeeded and that there was absolutely no damage to it or the payload.

Their phone conversations were not at all satisfactory. They definitely did better when face-to-face, she thought, remembering his eyes on hers, and his lips, too.

Now, coming out of the lodge and blinking in the brightness, feeling the snow globe inside the tote bag thump against her side as she walked toward Cooper's truck sitting down the hill from the lodge, Lacey's expectations began to rise again.

He stood there beside it, waiting. His eyes were hidden behind dark glasses, his expression unchanging as the children ran up to him.

"We got sixty miles of single lane on the interstate," he said, handing Anna up into the cab after Jon. "But after that should be smooth sailin'. We should be to your folks' place by midafternoon."

"Oh…good."

He reached out for Lacey's tote bag, and she handed it over to him. He threw it up into the cab, said, "We'd better get to it," and started around the truck.

In a flash she was really mad. She had given him a gift, and he had given her a gift, not to mention he had kissed her and held her. He had given her plenty of reason to have expectations.

"Cooper." With careful control, she gently closed the passenger door.

"Yeah?" At least his eyebrow rose up over his glasses.

Yeah? She said, "I want to thank you for the snow globe. I love it…it's beautiful." That was all she could think to say.

"Uh, you're welcome. Thanks for the buckle, too. It's really nice."

"You're welcome."

They stood there for a few seconds gazing at each other. She thought for a moment that he was going to say something more. But then he gave a sort of nod and continued around the truck.

Lacey got up into the passenger seat and slammed the door, just as Cooper was slipping into the driver's seat.

She was madder than a wet hen, and embarrassed about it. Digging into her tote bag, she located her sunglasses and jammed them on her face.

As the truck brought them ever closer to their destination, two things dominated her mind: greeting her father and saying goodbye to Cooper.

After the way she had acted, she felt really silly, and that made her act even stiffer. She was not a child. She knew about a lot of single men, especially truckers. They had women everywhere. It had only been one kiss—and even if it had been a really fiery kiss to her, maybe he kissed women like that all the time. The trip and then the storm had thrown them together in a fantasy world of close proximity. Giving her a gift was probably just getting caught up in the spirit of the holiday. Even if he had been having some sort of feelings for her, he had obviously changed his mind, which was his right, after all.

She felt so stupid as to almost cry, so she had to keep her face turned toward the passenger window.

The trip went perversely smoothly. For the first hour, confined to the one lane, driving was slowed, but when they hit the two lanes, Cooper got up to full speed. He had to stop three extra times for Anna to go to the bathroom, and they spent a lot of time serenaded by Christmas tunes on the radio and pacifying the two voices that kept asking, "Are we there yet?"

Lacey's nerves became tighter and tighter, so that when Cooper pulled the Kenworth off the highway exit for Pine Grove and asked which way, she fairly snapped at him.

"Just drop us over at that restaurant. I'll call my sister to come get us."

"Which way, Lacey?" he said in an exasperated tone.

"I'll call my sister."

"I'll take you."

He stared at her, and she stared back. Two pair of dark glasses staring each other down.

"Left," she said. "Five miles."

"Are we alll-most there, Ma-ma?" Anna said.

A lot had changed in Pine Grove in eleven years. Where she and Beth had once cut Christmas trees, a shopping mall had blossomed. Huffner's Country Market was now a Super Save and Fowler's TV Repair had become Fowler's Video Rental. Seeing this caused Lacey's spirits to sink even further, although this was actually an improvement, because she was distracted from her hurt over Cooper's lack of attention.

Soon, however, the Kenworth was rumbling its way slowly down the wide street of the graceful old neighborhood where Lacey had grown up. It appeared little changed. The trees were taller, the bushes thicker, but all fit her memory, she saw with relief. Although the big truck was definitely out of place, and Lacey worried about Cooper getting a ticket.

"Is this it?" Jon asked excitedly.

"Which one?" Anna said, craning her neck.

"There…" Lacey pointed, and Cooper came to a rolling stop at the curb in front of her parents' large sloping yard. The sameness of it all was heartily reassuring, and a little strange, too. Quite suddenly she felt nineteen again, as if all the years since had been wiped away.

She stared at the house, feeling as if she couldn't move, even when she saw the front door opening. Then people were stepping out onto the porch. Her parents…yes, it was them. Oh, her mother's hair was white. Her father… Why, he was bent.

When Cooper said, "I'll go up and speak to them," she could do nothing but gape at him in astonishment.

Ignoring Lacey's expression, Cooper got out of the truck, paused and gave his hair a quick swipe. He felt foolish. It was none of his business. But he didn't want the kids going up there and being rejected by their grandpa right in front of their faces. The memory of his own hurt caused him to stride toward the large brick house with firm, long steps.

He came to a stop, looked up at the porch and took quick inventory of the people staring at him—a stern, no-nonsense type of man with silver hair and deep creases on either side of his turned-down mouth, the woman stylish and petite and standing one step behind the man. A movement behind the curtains of the window indicated onlookers inside.

Cooper returned his gaze to the silver-haired man. "I've brought Lacey and your grandchildren for a visit." He watched the man's eyes grow small. "Will you welcome them?"

"Who are you?" the man asked after a long, silent moment.

"Just a friend," Cooper replied.

Another long pause in which the man's taut expression seemed to crumble. His eyes turned moist when he said, "Please ask my daughter and her children to come in."

"Yes, sir, I will."

Lacey saw Cooper return down the walkway in brisk steps. Her father, too, came forward on the porch and looked toward the truck.

She opened the door. The both dreaded and hoped-for moment had arrived, and she suddenly felt she couldn't cope with either. She about fell out of the cab, and then Cooper was there, offering his steadying hand and reaching to help Anna.

Then joy burst within Lacey, when her mother came hurrying down the walk with open arms.

"Mama!"

"My baby!"

The scent of Yardley's Lavender and the softness of silk were in her mother's hug. Her mother slipped away to Anna and Jon, and Lacey was left gazing up the path at her father, still waiting on the porch. She walked slowly toward him.

The same man, yet changed. The sternness was there, but softened with the frailty of age.

"Daddy…" She reached for Jon and Anna, taking refuge with them. "These are my children."

She couldn't remember ever seeing her father cry, but now a tear slipped down his cheek. Lacey blinked, her vision growing almost too blurry to see. When her father opened his arms, she rushed to embrace him, feeling his rough face against hers, his coarse silver hair.

"Oh, Daddy, I've missed you." And then she cried into his white dress shirt. Still the starched white dress shirts.

"Welcome home," her father said gruffly. He squeezed her tight, then, self-consciously averting his gaze, he pulled away and turned to the children, pure pleasure lighting his face. "So these are my grandchildren…."

Bedlam broke out, with Beth and her husband and children pouring from the house, everyone hugging and talking excitedly.

Suddenly Lacey remembered Cooper. Fearing he might have already slipped away, she looked around and saw him there, captured by her mother.

Emily Sawyer was never one to forget the propriety

of inviting a guest for refreshment. Cooper was trapped, because the older woman had him firmly by the arm.

Talking with Leon Sawyer, Cooper drank a third cup of coffee and finished off a second piece of pumpkin pie. He knew he had to get gone. The way Lacey kept looking at him—had been looking at him throughout the day—had him churned up inside, like a wildcat caught in a net.

He felt overwhelmed by the rest of the crowd, too. He had rarely been surrounded by a family like this, so many people, so much talking, and lots of questions about him—what he did and where he lived, and about family. That was a big one.

"Who are your people, Mr. Cooper?" Emily Sawyer asked in her cultured tone. She was what Cooper thought of as a real lady.

But he didn't understand the question and just stared at her.

"She means your family," Lacey interpreted. "Cooper's from Tennessee, Mama, but he was an only child, and his family is all gone."

"Oh." Emily Sawyer looked like she found this quite strange.

And Cooper felt a little strange, with the way everyone kept giving him those secretive looks.

Everyone except Leon, who looked at him as if he was trying to guess his coat size. Once Leon asked him how long he had known Lacey. Cooper could tell his answer didn't set too well with the man, who held strong views and was trying to hold them on his tongue.

Cooper saw the attachment between Lacey and her father, but he saw the personality clash, as well. Two stubborn people with opposite outlooks.

"Surely you'll stay for dinner," Emily Sawyer said. "We have plenty of leftovers from the big meal at noon today."

"No, thank you, ma'am. I have to get this haul up to Washington." He rose, looking around for his coat.

"But it's Christmas Day. Surely you can celebrate Christmas Day."

"Oh, I've had a good celebration," he said, catching a glimpse of Lacey's eyes on him. All of them were looking at him. "And I couldn't eat another bite on top of this good pie." He didn't want to appear rude.

Jon and Anna came with Lacey, walking Cooper out to his truck. Jon shook Cooper's hand, and then Anna lifted her arms for a hug.

Cooper was really struck by this. He bent down to her level, and her small arms went around his neck, as she said solemnly, "Goodbye, Cooper."

He couldn't say anything. He just gave her a squeeze.

Lacey then hurried the children back to the house. "Give me a minute alone with Cooper, you two." She watched them go up to the house, not at all certain of facing Cooper.

Finally she folded her arms close and slowly turned to him, seeing the colorful lights on the houses up and down the street, the sky overhead, the clear, crisp pale blue of evening.

"The clear sky means it'll be really cold tonight. It'll be clear for your drive to D.C., though."

"Yeah, should be an easy drive."

"I am very grateful for the ride out. I'm sorry for all the inconvenience." She searched his dark eyes for any encouraging sign that she might say something of the feelings pushing up into her throat.

"You didn't cause the snow," he said, reaching up and opening the cab door and tossing in his hat, as if eager to be on his way.

"I know you could have come ahead of that storm, had it not been for me and the children."

"We made it okay."

They gazed at each other for an awkward moment. Lacey was trying to get what she needed to say to her tongue, when he asked, "You want me to stop and get you next week for the ride back?"

"Do you want us to ride back with you?" Hope sprang ahead of all the other feelings.

But he gave a shrug, which was not a response she was seeking, and he said, "It's no problem for me. I'll just take a few local loads up around D.C. to fill the time. I'll be heading to Albuquerque anyway."

"I asked if you *wanted* us to come."

He stared at her, then shifted his stance. "Look… you're askin' me for somethin' I can't give, Lacey. I don't have it in me to give."

His words just broke her heart and made her furious at the same time. She couldn't accept it. She felt that she had to make him understand.

"You can't know that at this point," she said. "We don't know anything at this point, except there darn sure is something between us. I know I have feelin's for you. I'm not fool enough to say that I love you. I can't know that yet, but I do know that I *think* I'm halfway in love with you, and that's really something."

His gaze had shifted to her shoulder, yet still she said, "Maybe it's more what I can give you, Cooper. But you can't know, if you don't give it a chance."

Cooper shook his head, his eyes bleak. "Lacey, I'm just a burned-out old driver. You and me...we're like water and diesel fuel. We aren't gonna mix. You don't see things like they are, only like you want them to be. I'm not anything at all like what you think you're seein'. And life just doesn't turn out like that."

"Like what, Cooper? You don't think I can really love you? How can you know at this point?"

"Sometimes, Lacey, love won't change the facts. It didn't with your dad when he got angry and threw you out, did it?"

"It did when I came back."

"And there was a world of hurt in between."

Lacey shoved her fists into her coat pockets. He was determined to reject the idea of them having anything, and she was a fool to try to change his mind.

"Well, thanks so much for bringin' us," she said, stepping backward. "And for goin' up to check out Daddy for me." She wouldn't cry. She would die first. "We'll be fine. And we'll ride back on the bus."

Something flashed across his face—pain, maybe—and Lacey felt a slice of triumph and confusion.

"I'll see you back at Gerald's then," he said.

"Yes. See you then."

She did not stand there and watch the truck leave. But from inside the house, she heard the sound of the engine as it faded.

Late that night, when everyone was asleep, Lacey slipped down to the kitchen for a cup of warm milk. As she pulled the mug from the microwave, she heard her father's shuffling footsteps.

"Can't you sleep?" he asked, entering the kitchen.

She smiled. "No more than you."

Her father gazed at her a minute, scratching his head, then reached into the refrigerator for the milk carton.

"I'll make it, Daddy. Sit down. You're not supposed to stand on that leg." At his look, she said, "Beth told me about the problem with your veins."

"Please don't plague me like the others—nag me like they do, or pander to me, either." He sat at the table.

"I won't, Daddy. I came home to make up and to have my father again. And it was big of me, too." She was rewarded by his slow smile.

She hugged him, and he hugged back. She stayed there a long moment in his embrace, which felt at once wonderful and strange. Her father had so seldom hugged her as a child.

When she moved away to the microwave, her father said, "Are you being kept awake by thoughts of that young man who brought you here?"

The question surprised her. "Some, I guess." She deposited his cup in front of him and took a chair at the table.

"When you were younger," he said, "you never talked to me about the boys you liked." He took note of her expression. "Okay, I will admit that I would not have listened. I suppose it is a bit late to start?" He raised an eyebrow.

"Yes, Daddy, I think it is. I don't think I want to talk about men in my life, other than to say there are not any." He looked so disappointed that she touched his arm. "But I love you for the invitation."

As they drank their milk, he reached for the photo album she had given him, opened it, and asked questions about each picture, as if hungry to catch up on his grandchildren's lives.

"You doin' all right out there in New Mexico?" he asked her. "Do you make enough to support you and the kids?"

"We do okay. Yes, sometimes things are really tight, but we eat well and have a decent apartment in a friendly neighborhood." For the first time she realized that she was proud of how much she had made of her life. "I like waitressing, Daddy. I'm good at taking care of people that way. The kids have everything they need and plenty of extras. We're doin' okay."

"You have to think of the future, Lace. What if…" Seeing her expression, he stopped. "Well, if you'd like to come here to live, you would be welcome. I'd…I'd like it, Lacey."

The tone and inflection as he said her name touched her to the core. "Thanks, Dad. That means a lot."

They leaned their heads close and looked at the picture album together.

* * *

Sitting cross-legged on the bed, she ran the brush Jon had given her in long strokes through her hair. It was a lovely brush-and-comb set, yet what Lacey held most dear was the look of love on her son's face when he had presented it, a gift bought with his own hard-earned money. And little Anna had made a snowflake for Lacey at school and carried it all the way on the trip in a card that she had also made herself, with a drawing of Santa Claus. Oddly enough, Anna had drawn the Santa with a black coat, Lacey realized.

She gave thanks for the blessing of her two children, as she looked at the crystal ball snow scene Cooper had given her. She shook it and set it down, watching the snow fall gently onto the little tree.

Just then Anna came in the room. She had been to the store with her grandparents. She showed Lacey a dog collar that she had bought for her puppy. "Santa said I would get my puppy later, but I thought I would have it by now," she said, doubt slipping into her eyes for the first time since Christmas Eve. "Cousin Buddy says I did not see Santa, but we did, didn't we, Mama?"

"Yes, we did," Lacey said immediately and even though she knew she was digging a big hole for herself. Probably lots of kids had been scarred for life by this Santa Claus thing.

"Oh, what does a kid like Buddy know? I'm sure you will get your puppy. But, honey, we're goin' home on the bus, you know, and I imagine Santa found that out, so he will wait until we get home to bring your puppy." Right then and there she made up her mind that she would get that puppy for her daughter. And she knew a lot of men she could get to dress up like Santa and bring the puppy, too.

Jon entered as she spoke the last part. "Why aren't we goin' back with Cooper? I don't wanna go back on no bus."

Anna looked questioningly at her, too.

"I know that it won't be as much fun on a bus, but it's the way it has to be. Cooper…he has a schedule to keep."

Jon said, "He would have taken us. I know he would," and tromped from the room.

Anna wanted to know when they would be going home. She was ready. Lacey showed her on the calendar in her purse. Her daughter said, "Then I will have my puppy!" and went happily out of the room, admiring her dog collar.

Lacey, having something of a panic, took up the phone beside the bed and called back to Gerald's, where she spoke to Jolene and instructed her friend to go to the pound, or anywhere she could, and get a puppy. Then she talked to Gerald and arranged for him to show up in a Santa suit with the puppy on the evening they arrived home.

When she got off the phone, she sank down on the side of the bed and wondered if she had done the right thing in encouraging her daughter's belief in a fantasy. How would this help her daughter learn to cope with life's harsh realities? Would her daughter develop a deep distrust in her own mother for all this lying, no matter how well-meaning?

She once more lifted the snow globe and thought how she didn't care about any future problems. She wanted her daughter to enjoy the idea of Santa Claus as long as possible. Soon enough Anna would be a woman and have to face realities.

With this idea, Lacey put the snow globe away in her suitcase. She didn't need to keep looking at it. She was no longer a child.

Christmas Lights

Another winter storm came, dumping snow from North Carolina on up to Boston and stopping traffic for the better part of two days. Cooper, who had delivered his payload of computer printers in Washington, D.C. and picked up a load of televisions and video equipment, which had been stranded because a driver couldn't get through, had made it to delivery in Baltimore and then was stranded there. He figured it was as good a time as any to rest up and didn't worry about hurrying west again.

Down in Pine Grove, the citizens saw the most snow

in a decade. Children and adults with young spirits were thrilled, running outside as soon as possible to make snow angels and snowmen.

Jon and Anna spent several afternoons sledding with their cousins at a nearby hill, and Lacey and her sister, Beth, even joined in. Lacey's mother threw a party, inviting old friends and family. The snow encouraged long girl-talks between Lacey and Beth, companionable ones with her mother over coffee, and stubborn arguments with her father, although he did most of the arguing. Lacey managed to contain herself to listening. She thought that she was finally learning to be an adult.

Her father fumed when Lacey maintained that her and the children's home was in Albuquerque now. He would not understand why she did not now choose to come home to live, where it would be a lot easier for her.

"I think what you mean is where you would be able to direct me," she said.

"I would be here to help. So would your mother. What's so wrong with that?"

When she explained that she and the children had their own home out west, that she had a good job, good friends, that the children had their familiar school and friends, he pointed out her lack of money and security and, most of all, family.

"You and Mama can still help me. You are only a phone call away," she told him, to which he grumbled irritably.

He would help with money, he told her, and if she had any sense at all, she would take it.

"Then you can start by givin' me bus fare back," she said, her pride relieved by the opening to ask.

But her father then started to rave about how she had not adequately planned the trip, nor did she have a decent savings account.

"Oh, Leon, you didn't have any savings account at Lacey's age. And you kept lookin' at all those brochures of faraway places, like Houston and Dallas, because you wanted to get away from your father," her mother said.

Conversation stopped and all eyes turned toward Emily Sawyer.

"I do have opinions," she said. "I simply have never seen sense in shouting them."

Though she had gotten firm with herself about being a grown-up and not believing in fantasies anymore,

Lacey found herself repeatedly gazing out the window, imagining the maroon Kenworth rolling up the street. She couldn't quite let Cooper go, in the way it was hard to let Christmas go and one kept the tree up and lights going every night.

One evening Beth found her at the front window. "Are you hopin' he'll come back?"

"No, not really…oh, maybe I imagine a little bit, but I barely know him. It's just silly."

"You seemed to know him pretty well to me. You've been waitin' on him for years, and you came clear across country with him." Beth flopped on the couch. "And I don't think it's silly. Lots of people have fallen in love in a matter of days."

"Who that you know?"

"This lady at the library. She went for a vacation in Cancun and came back with a husband."

"You are makin' that up."

"Well, not entirely. She came back next to engaged, and she did marry him. People do fall in love quickly."

"And they fall out of love quickly, too."

"Your point being?"

Lacey shook her head but resisted comment.

"Oh, just because things didn't turn out well with Shawn doesn't mean you couldn't fall in love with Cooper in a matter of days. And he could change his mind, too," Beth persisted. "He could think about what he's missin' and come back."

Lacey bent and prodded the fire with the poker. "It would be more probable for it to snow in July. Cooper isn't like that."

"It has snowed in July," Beth stated. "In Vermont, I believe, back in the eighteen-hundreds. So you see, miracles do happen. Besides, I thought you said you hardly knew him. How do you know, then, that he isn't like that?"

"Oh, I don't know what he might do. But it isn't like some passionate song or romantic story. I guess those things might really happen, but it isn't anything I can imagine for myself. I don't even want to. How I see me with Cooper is more real. He's reliable, for one thing. I feel safe and solid around him."

Then, more thoughtfully, "What I think happened to me with him is that I suddenly saw that I could actually be attracted to a man. I felt like a woman for the first time since…well, since I don't know when. Maybe ever. I had set aside any thought of a man in my life. The kids have taken everything I had. But now, I guess now I kind of hope that someone will come along."

"Then it would be just as well to hope for the guy that's already in the lead," Beth said, giving a grin.

"I think I'm too afraid of such a hope. I know there isn't a Santa Claus for grown women," Lacey whispered.

"Now, who told you that lie?" Beth said righteously. "Honey, if you are gonna hope, you might as well hope for exactly what you want. That's how it works."

Lacey tried to smile for her sister, who was lovingly and loyally trying to make her feel better.

"Let's take down the tree. Christmas is over," she said.

Cooper pulled off the highway at a rest stop outside of Richmond. He walked around the flatbed trailer load of axles he had picked up in Baltimore, checking the tie-downs. Hearing a shout, he looked over to see a rest stop maintenance worker toss aside something. A second maintenance worker swore and went after it—it was a little dog, which went right under Cooper's rig.

The two men came running over, one of them saying, "The damn thing peed on me. I ain' holdin' on to no peein' dog."

The other one had knelt down and called to the dog.

Cooper looked under, too. The dog had lain down. It was only a little puppy, and it looked half starved.

"People drop 'em out here all the time," the one man said to Cooper. "Fred...go get that chicken you had for lunch."

The puppy was easily lured by the food, and the man grabbed it up by the back of the neck, causing it to cry out, and didn't even give it the chicken.

Cooper, standing there watching for some reason, saw the man go to throw the little animal over into the dump bed of the maintenance truck like so much garbage.

"Hey!" he hollered out.

"Yeah."

"I'll take it." He strode toward the man. "Give it here. I'll take it."

"He's yours. Let him pee on you." The man tossed the dog at Cooper, who caught it and then had to hold it out from him, as it dribbled and whimpered.

Then, with a deep breath, he held the trembling animal close, wondering what in the world he had been thinking.

Standing there and watching the maintenance truck

drive off and feeling helpless, his gaze fell on the Dumpster at the end of the drive. He went over to see if he could find a box to hold the puppy. The Dumpster lid was heavy with snow. He had to clear it with one arm in order to open it.

Right inside was a surprising sight. A basket of a perfect size just sitting there, as if waiting for him.

Cooper felt called on to look upward. Was something going on here? he asked silently.

He pulled out the basket and plopped the puppy inside of it. And then he spied a McDonald's sack that still had most of a hamburger in it, too.

He headed the big rig down the road, with the puppy, now happily fed and curled atop a towel inside the basket. He knew very well he was heading for Pine Grove, and he argued with himself about it all the way. It was probably too late. She might already be on the bus back to Albuquerque. She might have met up with an old boyfriend. She probably wouldn't even be interested anymore, and if she wasn't, he was going to be stuck with the stupid puppy that had chewed holes in one of his good leather gloves.

He wanted a cigarette badly, which did not help his mood.

Night had fully come when his headlights fell on the exit sign for Pine Grove, and right at that same moment a country song came floating out from the radio, "Only Here For A Little While."

Swearing under his breath, he turned down the exit ramp and pulled to the side at the bottom, stopped the truck, got out and strode to the front, where he worked at the front grille, while his fingers grew numb with cold. The passengers in a number of cars looked at him, wondering at the actions of a man who seemed really mad about something.

He got back into the truck, thinking that he might have been able to save himself a lot of trouble if he had had a phone number for her.

A sound drew Lacey's attention from the game of chess that she was playing with her father. She shifted in order to see out the window.

Lights? She had thought of him so much that she was sure she was imagining things, but she got up to go look.

Her eyes fell on the truck, the glimmer of maroon beneath the street lamp. *Cooper?*

She turned and stared at her father. "It's Cooper."

"Well, don't just stand there. You had better get on out to see what he's come for." Her father urged her with gestures. "Go on!"

She hurried to the door, flung it open, and then she was running down the walk. Halfway down she stopped. *Maybe he had not come back for her. Maybe she had left something in his truck, or he had to tell her something.*

He appeared in front of the truck. When he saw her, he stopped, too.

Lacey waited, her heart pounding.

Slowly he walked toward her. Then faster, walking with *anticipation!*

She flung herself at him, and he caught her hard against him, and it was "Lacey…Lacey," and "Cooper… Cooper," and they were kissing and touching and searching each other's eyes.

"I don't know what's happened to me," Cooper said in such a tone that she had to laugh out loud.

"You don't sound happy about it."

He looked at her as if he could eat her up. It amazed her. She had not bargained for that.

He said, "I just know I couldn't leave without you and the kids. Yes, even the kids." He gave a hoarse chuckle, then frowned down at her. "Will you go back with me, Lacey? Can we…can we see about us? No promises," he cautioned. "I don't know about any of this. I…"

"Oh, Cooper," she interrupted him, laughing at once. "What's happenin' to you is love, darlin'." She wound her arms around his neck. "And I think I love you," she whispered just before his lips crushed hers in a hot kiss.

When at last he lifted his head, Lacey had to gasp for breath. Her mind whirled with the wonder of it all.

The next instant he was tugging her along.

"What in the world…"

"I have something to show you." He was as excited as a child. He tugged her to the front of the Kenworth. "Look."

The Christmas lights on the grille. They no longer said, *Bah Humbug.*

H-O-squiggle-*O*-squiggle-*O*. Why, it said *Ho, Ho, Ho,* if one was imaginative.

"I had trouble with the *H*s," Cooper said.

Lacey, tears of joy streaming down her face, said, "You believe." She felt almost ashamed at how easily she had given up on such belief.

Cooper grinned gently. "Yeah, well, I guess I do. I

sure couldn't let the other stay, with Anna ridin' in the truck."

There came a yipping, drawing their attention to the windows, where the puppy bobbed up and down.

"Oh, yeah…Santa sent Anna's puppy by way of me." He felt about ten feet tall at the way Lacey regarded him.

Epilogue

The events of that Christmas became so precious to Lacey and Cooper that they put off their wedding until the following Christmas, wanting to have the ceremony at what they now looked on as their own magical season.

In the years that have followed, as the holidays roll around, each season is made more precious by the sweet reminiscing of that first that brought them together. Cooper claims that Lacey's deviousness holds them together, because it had been her plan to sneak the puppy around to her parents' back porch. Emily Sawyer had jumped in with the plan and put a note from Santa in the basket with the dog, who only halfway ate it.

In the morning, when Anna found the puppy, she kept saying, "He's just like I imagined! Santa didn't forget! And he must have found out we were going back with Cooper, right, Mama?"

She promptly named the puppy Skippy.

Cooper felt thoroughly satisfied in the face of Anna's delight, and at the way Lacey, Jon and the others regarded him. He had told them about how he had rescued the puppy, which had not been so unusual, and how he had also found the perfect basket, which Lacey told him she felt was actually a dog basket. The finding of the basket at that same place was a little unusual, but stranger things had happened.

In fact, a stranger thing did happen three weeks later, when upon searching Anna's suitcase, trying to find some lost clothes, Lacey came upon not only a pair of pink Tuesday panties, but a folded piece of construction paper. On the paper was a childish drawing of a puppy in a basket. The puppy looked just like Skippy, a tan hound dog with a long tail and a flopped-over ear.

Lacey showed the paper to Anna and all of them at the supper table that night, and complimented her on the drawing. "But, honey, why did you put it in the suitcase? It deserves to be on the refrigerator."

"Because I wanted to keep it on our trip," Anna answered.

This puzzling answer led to more questions, and the surprising discovery that Anna had drawn the picture of the puppy on Christmas Eve, after their rescue by Santa Claus, to whom she had described what sort of puppy she wanted, and who had told her to draw a picture of the puppy she wanted with the crayons and paper he had given her as gifts that night.

It was Jon who put in, "She did draw it. I remember her doin' it." He looked at Cooper and Lacey with round eyes.

They never told Anna who had brought the puppy, and eventually they rather forgot about Cooper finding him. The tale became firmly—and perhaps truthfully, Lacey thought—that Santa had brought him.

Eventually Anna grew up and the belief in Santa faded, as it does with adults who tend to believe only what they see.

However, every time she saw a storefront Santa Claus, something would stir in her heart. And deep down, she knew the very true truth is that what exists in the heart is the most real thing of all.

* * * * *

Keep the magic going.
Turn the page for a sample of
Curtiss Ann Matlock's
LOST HIGHWAYS
available from MIRA books.

I'll Know When I Get There

A faded red car came up the entry ramp on her right. A little pissant economy job that looked as if it had been through the wringer. The driver door was primer gray. Giving out a puff of black smoke, it pulled right over in front of her.

Highly annoyed, Rainey thought that the driver obviously did not know the foremost rule of the road, which was that the biggest vehicle had the right of way. She would have moved over to make room for the little red car, but there was an eighteen-wheeler coming up on her left that would, she was fairly certain, mow her down without compunction.

Her nerves went to twanging as she came up on the little car that seemed incapable of gaining speed. It had a fluffy pillow in the back window…no, it was a cat and a tennis shoe. The cat's head came up, its eyes widened, and it fled.

She tapped her brakes, harder and harder, to keep from running over the car, and she imagined her mare, her mother's mare, back in the trailer, trying to suck her hooves on the floor in order to stay on her feet.

The eighteen-wheeler moved on ahead, leaving room for Rainey to pull into the left lane. Looking at the open road ahead with satisfaction, she began to press the accelerator.

The next instant, to her immense surprise and alarm, the little red pissant car pulled to the left, right in front of her again. The only reason she could come up with for this erratic move was that the driver felt the need to try out both lanes before settling on one.

Hands gripping the steering wheel, she again tapped the brake. She pictured running up on the little car's bumper and pushing. If her sister Charlene had been beside her, she would have been saying, "Now, Rainey...now, Rainey."

Charlene accused Rainey of being an aggressive driver. "Road rage. It's the epidemic of the modern age," Charlene said. "I saw all about it on CNN, and you've got it."

"I don't have rage.... Don't blow annoyance at inconsiderate drivers into rage. I am a considerate driver and expect others to be so. That's not too much to ask, if you ask me."

Maneuvering back to the right, she pressed the accelerator more forcefully this time and edged ahead while keeping a sharp eye on the faded red car for further signs of foolish behavior. She was ready to repel the little car if necessary.

Like a big ocean liner, her diesel truck took a bit to pick up speed, but once it got going, it really went down the road. She glanced in the side mirror and saw the little red card fighting the buffeting winds in the wake of her passing. She felt a little guilty. It might have been inconsiderate of her to pass so quickly that she blew him off the road.

Leaving the little car behind, she headed on down the interstate highway out of San Antonio, breezing along with the sedans and semis and Winnebagos in her mother's old dingy-white Ford one-ton pickup truck and the matching gooseneck horse trailer with the name Valentine painted in flowing turquoise across each side.

The truck and trailer were both twelve years old, and for the first years her mother had driven the dog out of them. The truck was on its second engine, and that had nearly a hundred thousand miles on it. The air conditioner worked when it took a notion, which it did not right then, so she had the windows down, allowing the warm, end-of-the-day wind to blow her hair and bat her silver feather earrings. The sun visor no longer stayed in any one place. When not in use, it had to be wedged up with a piece of wood, and when in use, it wobbled so that the sun's rays blinked at her. It was quite disconcerting. Driving into the western sun, as she was doing at that moment, she would sit up straight and dodge and bob, trying to keep the best position behind the visor, which kept rapidly changing, since she was going nearly seventy-five miles an hour down the highway.

She had been driving the rig for over a month, and it was her name on the title now, but she still considered it her mother's truck and trailer. Her mother's ragged brown sweater and faded lavender satin pillow were tucked behind the seat, and she still hadn't brought herself to clean out her mother's classic Jim Reeves and Patsy Cline cassette tapes from the console, nor had she removed the pocket New Testament and wad of napkins— the two things Mama always referred to as her "emergency kit"—from the glove box. They would pop out like a jack-in-the-box every time it was opened, as if to remind her of their presence. *Here, save your soul and wipe your greasy hands at the same time,* sort of like Mama was still watching over her.

Once she cut her finger, and the first thing she grabbed were napkins from that wad. After that she was careful to replenish the wad with two extra each time she stopped for a meal.

She had even returned to her maiden name of

Rainey Valentine. It was easier than making the explanations that ended up sounding so tawdry.

Just then, despite her own top rate of speed, a pale pink Cadillac with Mary Kay in pink script on the side window came flying past. Drivers in Texas didn't waste time.

The cotton-candy-haired woman at the wheel of the Cadillac tooted and waved. She had obviously seen the Mary Kay bumper sticker on the back door of the horse trailer.

Rainey returned the wave happily in the camaraderie of the road and Mary Kay users.

How her mother had put so many miles on the truck was by traveling all over Oklahoma, Texas, Kansas and a few points beyond, selling Mary Kay cosmetics and riding barrel races. That could be considered something of an unusual combination, but it didn't seem unusual next to the fact that Mama had raced barrels and sold Mary Kay until the age of seventy-five.

On the back of the horse trailer Mama had stuck a collection of bumper stickers. Along with the one touting Mary Kay, there was one for each state to which she had traveled to barrel race. There was one for the American quarter horse, another for barrel horses and another that said, Cowboy Up. One said Love from Valentine. Below that were the ones that said, Trust in the Lord, and Honk if You Love Jesus. Then there was the one that said, American by Birth, Southern by the Grace of God.

Charlene thought the conglomeration of bumper stickers was tacky, and Rainey had to agree with her.

"Lots of people might start botherin' you for the Mary Kay, and you don't sell it," Charlene pointed out. "And that Southern saying is in poor taste. Somebody might pick a fight with you over it. I always worried about that with Mama, but you couldn't tell her anything. You ought to go ask Freddy to have the boys down in his body shop get them off," Charlene suggested.

Freddy was their older brother; he owned the only Ford dealership for fifty miles.

Rainey didn't care for the idea. "If they're taken off, there will be all these rectangle places all over. I'd need to get the trailer painted, and then the truck would look awful next to it."

She wasn't going to touch those bumper stickers.

For one thing, Freddy most likely would make her pay for the job. Freddy was not noted for his generosity, and on top of that, he considered her the spoiled late child who had always been given too much.

Removing the stickers herself would have been a major undertaking and would have ruined her fingernails, about which she was quite particular. And despite their being so tacky, she rather liked those bumper stickers. They seemed a testament to Mama, who had died in the spring, suddenly, of heart stoppage.

Heart failure was what the doctor said, but Rainey rejected that term. Her mother's heart had never in this world failed. When people said that Coweta Valentine's death had come as a surprise, she would think of how her mother would have laughed about that. Her mother had been eighty-two, and she would often say, "When I kick the bucket." When people would try to hush this kind of talk, she would say, "The one sure thing is that a person starts dyin' soon as they're born. Why, dyin' is a part of livin', might as well get used to it."

Her mother had lived more thoroughly than anyone Rainey had ever known. And what Freddy said was true—Rainey *had* been her mother's favorite, her late child, and the one closest to her.

Mama always said that Rainey was her twin soul, and Daddy said Mama carried on whole conversations with her from the time she was in the womb. She and Mama would finish up each other's sentences, driving Daddy and Freddy wild, and call each other at the same exact moment, so that their phone lines connected without ringing.

She was the one who knew the instant Mama was stricken. She had thumped the bottle of Glyco-Thymoline she had been pricing down on the counter and listened, just as if hearing someone call her name. Then, hollering to Mr. Blaine as she ripped off her white coat, "I think somethin's wrong with Mama," she had dashed out of the drugstore like the wildly alarmed woman that she was, running the entire four blocks to her parents' big home and around back to the little apple orchard, to find her mother lying on the moist ground, holding her chest and whispering desperate, shocking things, until Rainey had said, "Shut up, Mama, and hang on."

She had thought at the time that her mother had

been out of her mind with pain and talking crazy. It was later, during her mother's final hours, that she was faced with the profound shock that what her mother said was true fact.

The picture of her mother clinging to life and to one final ordering of everyone else's lives returned to her again and again—her mother lying in the hospital bed, her father holding her mother's hand, Freddy looking from their parents to Rainey, and Charlene sobbing loudly over by the doorway. In this memory she would see her mother's mouth moving, revealing the shameful secret, but Rainey truly did not hear a sound, except for Charlene's sobbing.

Mostly Rainey found any of it too painful to think about.

As original in death as in life, their mother had skipped over their father and left all she owned to her children. Coweta Valentine had been listed as one-eighth Chickasaw on the rolls, although she had argued for years that she was one-fourth. The old Indian way was to trace the blood lineage through the women rather than the men. It was figured that the mother of a child was certain, whereas exactly who was the father was not. This was a practicality that had seemed to escape a number of societies in this world, as well as turning out particularly apt in Coweta Valentine's case, Rainey thought a number of times.

Charlene got the family Bible, dating from the mid-1800s and listing births in Mississippi, before the great Indian hater Andrew Jackson (history books said Indian fighter, but Mama always vehemently corrected the term) forced the family off their land and out west, a pair of earrings said to have come from Georgia gold, and the old house and acreage on Church Street, even though their daddy remained alive and living there. Daddy had his own money, but he really didn't have many belongings. Mama had trusted Charlene and the rest of them to take care of Daddy.

Freddy, the eldest and only son, was pretty upset about Charlene getting the house. Although he had received the bulk of his mother's portfolio, he felt the house, one of the grandest in town, with a cupola and wraparound porch, five acres of lawn, orchard and corral, and a border of lilacs, should have been his. No doubt he thought it fitted his station as owner of the Ford dealership, and his wife Helen thought this even more. Helen was all the time throwing dinner parties, and Rainey imagined Helen saw herself having parties out across the porch, the kind with Chinese lanterns and waiters in black tie, although God knew where she'd get them.

"I am not about to move out of my modern home into that big old museum," Charlene told Freddy in the firm way she had of talking with her hand on her hip. "Joey's spurs would gouge the floors in no time."

Charlene's husband Joey was a professional horse trainer. His spurs never came off his boots, and when his boots went on in the morning, they didn't come off until he went to bed. Charlene worshiped her wool wall-to-wall carpet because of this. She was also a walking advertisement for heat pumps and modern insulation.

"You and Helen can live there when Daddy's done with it," Charlene assured Freddy, then added, "Of course, I'll keep the deed."

Rainey's inheritance had been mama's truck and horse trailer, her old barrel racing mare Lulu, and her considerable stock of Mary Kay cosmetics. There were probably enough cosmetics to last a lifetime, which was a pretty good thing, because Rainey had always enjoyed makeup. Nature had been good to her, but nature does often require a helping hand.

She guessed her mother had wanted her to have at least some small security for life all the way around, because she also left her oil leases that currently brought in nearly eight hundred dollars a month. This income would go up drastically if those Mideast countries got crazy again.

Oh, Freddy'd had a lot to say about that. "She'll piss it away like she has everything else. Mama should have let me take care of it for her."

Freddy looked at Rainey, and everyone else, with more scorn than usual during the weeks following their mother's death, while Charlene loved everyone more than ever, and their daddy went along in his silent sorrow.

As the days passed, the length and breadth of their loss sunk in. Their beloved wife and mother, who had always been there with a ready ear and wise answers and strong, loving arms, was gone.

For Rainey's daddy, this meant that his wife would

never again warm her cold feet on his thighs or yell at him to take his cigarette out on the porch, put his vitamins in his hand or find his discarded jacket.

For her and her brother and sister, it was a stark reminder that they were no longer children. It meant that they now carried around a permanent empty hole in their hearts, that they had to solve their own problems, and that they had taken their place in line for old age and death.

Her daddy spent a lot of the first month of his widowhood rocking on the front porch. Rainey knew this because she went over to clean for him and to make certain that he got at least one hot meal a day. It seemed as if all life had gone out of him. He looked like a deflated bag of skin rocking there. He didn't say more than five words to her on any one day.

Then one morning barely four weeks after Mama had left them, Rainey went over and found widowed Mildred Covington sitting with her daddy, and words were pouring out of his plumping up body. It was like with every breath he took to speak, his body filled a little more.

Five weeks after Mama died, Freddy broke off with

the girlfriend no one was supposed to know about and took up taking Helen to the Main Street Café for breakfast each morning and sitting beside her on the pew of the Southern Baptist Church each Sunday.

Charlene started looking in the mirror and crying because she was turning forty-five, and then she began to pester Joey when he came in from work, dragging him into the bedroom in a desperate attempt to hold the years at bay by trying for a fourth baby.

Rainey looked into the mirror, too, playing with all the Mary Kay, and she saw a woman who was almost thirty-five, twice divorced, had lost the only child she had ever conceived, and was living in a forty-year-old run-down farm cottage behind her sister's house. Gazing back at her from every plate glass store window she passed was a lost woman who did not know who she really was, nor where she belonged.

A few false starts will make you stronger, her mother had told her a number of times.

"How many of those, Mama? How many mistakes and wasted years? What if I never get it right?"

Her mother was not there anymore to give the perfect answers.

Rainey did as much crying as Charlene, but there was only her own pillow to soak up the tears.

After about a week of crying, she got out and washed and waxed her mother's legacy of the truck and trailer. She very carefully waxed a second time around the bumper stickers, and then she loaded up Mama's eighteen-year-old mare and took off to race barrels. It was the only action she could think to take.

She and Mama had raced barrels together the entire time she was in high school and until she'd gone off to college, where she had met and married Robert, who had considered any horse activity other than the Kentucky Derby the preoccupation of the lower classes. From that time on, she never really got into the sport again. She guessed she'd stayed too busy trying to earn a living and deal with her second husband, Monte. Later she guessed she'd just been too busy dealing with regrets.

Thinking back in the despondent manner one always falls into after a loved one dies, Rainey felt so many regrets and questions. Racing barrels gave her something to do in which she could lose her grief and confusion, and at the same time connect to her mother.

Also, racing barrels gave her somewhere to drive *to* and *away from* home. Something to make her forget the pain of lost years behind, the confusion of present life, and the fright of the uncertainties in life ahead.

She got so caught up in this endeavor that she finally quit her job at Blaine's Drugstore and took off to travel the rodeo circuit for the remaining weeks of summer.

"Just where are you goin' with this, Little Bit?"

Her daddy always called her "Little Bit." Directly on quitting her job, she had driven over to tell him her intentions. She had found him watering her mother's fragrant old garden roses.

"I don't know, Daddy," she said, her voice coming hoarse and stammering. "I guess I just need to get away...you know, have time to myself to sort things out. And I like racing. I want to do somethin' I like."

Daddy nodded. He never had much of an expression, and he didn't now. Disappointment sent her spirit slipping out her toes.

He asked her to pull more hose for him, and she did that, then she went in to check his refrigerator, thinking that she might need to go grocery shopping for him before she took off. The refrigerator was full of fruit salad and cottage cheese and skim milk and a plate of shredded barbequed roast. She figured it was Mildred Covington's work.

Staring at all the shiny plastic-wrapped dishes, she felt a sad sense of fading away, turning invisible.

Daddy came in and said he had a couple of things for her. He went upstairs and came back with two cardboard boxes.

He said, "Since you're goin' travelin', you can take this one over to your Aunt Lillabel in Ardmore. It's the silver brush and comb from your mama's dresser. She always said Lillabel should have it, and this one is the mystery books your mama had meant to send to your cousin Rowan down in Waco. You get by both those places. Like as not there'll be rodeoin' somewhere around them."

He looked at her for a moment before breaking the gaze. She knew he was trying to give her places to go to be with people she knew. Between them, her mother and father had an enormous family scattered all over Oklahoma and Texas.

As she started to leave, her father cleared his throat and said, "Rainey, don't you worry about not knowin' where you're goin'. I imagine you'll know when you get there."

Greatly surprised, she looked up to see him again averting his gaze and taking out his handkerchief to mop his face.

"Thanks, Daddy," she said. Very hesitantly, she dared kiss his cheek, closing her eyes and sucking in the dear, familiar scent of him, of Old Spice and tobacco and earth.

He grabbed her hard then, about startling her socks off. He crushed her against his chest, smashing the cigarette pack in his pocket and burying her nose into his salty neck. For a moment he held her tight, and she clung to him.

Then he let go and turned away. Her vision blurred and her throat nearly swelled shut, Rainey watched him walk out the back door, stiff and bent, weighed down by such a cloud of sorrow.

"Have you lost your *mind?*" Charlene wailed.

Rainey must have interrupted her sister and Joey

when she had called to announce her leaving, because Charlene was clutching around her what appeared to be one of Joey's denim shirts, and it could have been all she had on. This shocked Rainey; Charlene had always been the one to hold tight to decorum.

She said, "I guess I have, but I think that I did it a long time ago," and turned to throw her bags into the back of the truck. She didn't want Charlene to see her tears, or her shock. Keeping her face averted, she slipped in behind the wheel, while Charlene hollered through the window.

"Oh, Rainey, would you just quit bein' so dramatic? What are you gonna live on? You ain't good enough at barrels to earn any kind of money, and eight hundred dollars a month sure hasn't made you independently wealthy, you know."

"Lulu and I made a hundred dollars last weekend."

She didn't like Charlene having the idea that she and Lulu were the bottom of the barrel, so to speak. Maybe they weren't about to take the finals by storm, but they had begun to place about every other go.

"Oh, that's gonna pay for a day's fuel and meals and motel," Charlene said sarcastically.

"I'm only takin' off for a month or two, and I imagine I won't be stayin' in a lot of motels," she told her sister, gazing out the windshield while she spoke. "The first place I'm goin' is over to Aunt Lillabel's. I have to make a delivery for Daddy. I'll call you every few days. I'll always let you know where I am, in case you need me for anything."

She said that, but she couldn't foresee that anyone would need her. Mildred Covington pretty well had Daddy covered, and Helen was over there a lot now, keeping things up so they would be in prime condition when she got to move in, whether in one year or twenty. Freddy had Helen, and Charlene had Joey and the kids. Rainey was the odd man out, so to speak.

Charlene raked back her hair and said, "Rainey, I know…well, we're all pretty unsettled right now. But it is only the shock. It will straighten out in time."

She supposed that her sister was trying to be Mama for her, but she and Charlene had never been particularly close, and right then was not an opportune time to start.

"I imagine so. I'll call you from Aunt Lillabel's."

As she started away, Charlene surprised her by running alongside the truck, sobbing and yelling at her not to be stupid and that Mama would be upset.

Rainey doubted Mama would have been upset. Mama had left upset behind.

And she didn't know what to do. She saw Charlene's shapely pale legs catch the sunlight and her bare feet step lightly on the grass and gravel. She was a little afraid Charlene was going to fall down, or possibly throw herself in front of the truck. She would have simply outrun her sister, but she didn't think it would be very nice to stir dust in her face.

"Rainey, you can't run away from yourself, you know!"

Rainey thought maybe she could try.

"Where in the world are you goin'?" Charlene finally came to a stop, stamping one bare foot.

"I don't know," Rainey called back to her, "but

I'm goin' somewhere, and I guess I'll know when I get there."

As she turned onto the county road, she decided not to even tell Freddy she was going.

With one quick glance in the rearview mirror, she left Valentine behind.